HEALING JOURNEY

Published by:

EYE MVP Publishers

[South Africa - Free State, Botshabelo]

Published in [South Africa]

ISBN [978-0-7961-8417-7]

Cover design by [EYE MVP PUBLISHERS]

Interior design by [EYE MVP PUBLISHERS]

© Author [Blandile Nicol Vuyiswa]

First edition

[2024]

TABLE OF CONTENTS

INTRODUCTION

My name is Vuyiswa Nicol Blandile from South Africa - Free State province in a town called Botshabelo. I am a novelist, I never dreamed that I would become a writer, but when I started writing, I couldn't stop. I have always been passionate about family love - the importance of family love is often the foundation of our lives, and it can be the source of our greatest joys and deepest sorrows. In this book, I will explore the ways in which family love can shape our lives, for better or for worse.

I hope to shed light on the importance of maintaining healthy and loving relationships with our family members, even in the face of difficult circumstances. So, I decided to write this book to share my knowledge and experience with others. In this book I will explore many facts of heartbreak, betrayal, love and mostly forgiveness. I hope my stories can take readers on a journey to new worlds and new possibilities. I hope readers enjoy my book, learn something and inspire them.

DEDICATION

I dedicate this book to all couples out there who can strive together through thick and thin. Then mostly dedicated to my loving parents, my beautiful caring mom Madiile Suzan Blandile and my charming angel, my late father Balekile Thomas Blandile for their love and support. For always encouraging me to pursue my passion and follow my dream. Not to forget my grandfather Motsamai Abele Masiu for always being my pillar of strength.

ACKNOWLEDGEMENT

I was inspired by novel writer like Ivan Turgenev and poet like Engelinah Masiu. I would like to express my deepest gratitude to my beloved family and friends who have supported me throughout this journey. Without their belief in me and their words of encouragement I would not have been able to achieve this precious goal.

Special thanks to author Bangtar The MVP whom has always been my biggest cheerleader, for his guidance and wisdom. Not to forget my sisters Mathapelo Amanda Masiu, Thandeka Irene Blandile and Noscelo Judith Mzala, whom they had always been my sounding board.

I am highly grateful for their love and support.

SYNOPSIS

Matty is the epitome of resilience and a phenomenal woman. Living with her mum, a sister-cousin, and a father who died before he could see her achievements, she went through a period of depression after his death but came out victorious. Having graduated from the University of Johannesburg, she became a teacher before changing her career to business. Matty has several businesses to her name, including one with her husband. However, she experienced personal tragedy when she lost her firstborn child before delivery. In romance, she was first happily married but later experienced infidelity by her partner and finally discovered love and fulfillment once again. As she shares her journey, more about her new love will be revealed. Get ready to watch her story with a cup of tea.

CHAPTER 1

It was Thursday in the afternoon, I was coming from school, seeing my half-sister crying made me happy that day because I've always wanted to be the only child.

Well, she's my mom's daughter meaning I am the second daughter, but I was the first and the last to my father. Her coming to stay with us made me feel as if my mom does not love me anymore.

I passed her without greeting, I entered the house, full of the neighbors and everyone was crying. I greeted everyone and went to the rest room to take off my uniform. Usually before taking off the uniform, I go greet my dad in his room. He was very sick, seeing him lying there on his dead bed unable to do anything was very painful. But that day I went straight to my bedroom.

While taking off the uniform I heard wheels running as it was the hospital bed or something, I came out of the room to check what was happening. Little did I know that being happy about someone's sorrow was actual being happy about my sorrow.

It was my dad taken by Diner. I just stared at him; I couldn't cry, nor could I talk. I went back to the rest room to finish taking off the uniform. After getting dressed up I went outside sat next to his car, switched my phone on and played "I can't live if living is without you " by Mariah Carey.

After few minutes I got up and went to my mom's uncle's (Grandma Grace) house but the was no one at home, despite no one's respond I kept on knocking because my mind was elsewhere. On my way to the gate, I saw one of my grandma Graces sons walking with Sis Bee and her husband, I went to him running. His name was Thembi Khuzwayo. I asked him where his mom is, told me she isn't around and for couple of weeks.

I hugged him and cried my heart out. They starred at each other and asked me what's wrong. I had to start from the beginning and tell them what happened, well I did.

"I came back from school, and I found everyone crying, after few minutes when I got in my room, I heard wheels sound, I went outside to check that when I saw him covered meaning he was dead."

They gave me sad faces and trust me I felt their condolences. Thembi rushed to his house and grabbed the keys. On our way Sis Bee and her husband tagged along. We all went to my place, when we reached there, they went inside, and I stayed outside.

That day suddenly everything became impossible, life introduced a new shift in my heart. It was a sudden change a sudden shift. Thinking of the memories I created with him, tears kept falling down my cheeks.

The funeral was the following week, everyone prepared for the funeral. For the moment it felt great to meet all my cousins and other family members. The funeral passed and everyone left. The house started to feel empty, it was so quiet. From that time, I've started spending time all alone because the only friend I had left the world. I then became depressed; anxiety became my middle name and loneliness was my best friend.

On Monday after lunch at school Mam Buthelezi came to talk to me. she was my teacher. She was the best teacher every kid could ask for.

"Hi" it was Miss Buthelezi

"Hy mam." I said.

"How are you holding up." She said.

 "I am good mam can I help you." I said

Said that with attitude.

"Well, we have counselling for kids like..." I stood up and interrupted.

"Kids like what? Do I look sick to you, Do I look mad?" I said.

"No listen to me, I am trying to help you. Ever since your father passed on you haven't been yourself. You aren't even doing good in your schoolwork. You are so young to let this drown you, you're only 10 years old." She said.

"Well, I did not ask for your help." I said.

"I know but try this counselling once." She said.

"Do you know how it feels to lose a father? Huh! NO, you don't so please leave me alone." I said.

With my crying face I took my books and went to the washroom. I closed the door and screamed my heart out. I bet everyone near the toilets heard me. I fainted and was hospitalized for a very long time. Like I said before; I then became depressed, anxiety became my middle name and loneliness was my best friend. I stayed at Psychiatric hospital for almost a year.

FEW MONTHS LATER.

After I have fully recovered, I went home. At Psychiatric hospital was not that bad though everyone thinks am crazy, but I know am not. I was given time to study, also attended online classes. They really helped me because I won't have to wait for next year to go back to school. I got off my bed and wore my slippers made my way to my mom's room.

I knocked, entered the room, and sat next to her. My Mom was so beautiful, she was dark in complexion, had long afro hair, bit chubby but sexy, she also had dimples and big eyes. She was wearing her brown blouse with jeans, relaxing on her bed. I told her that I want to go back to school, can't tell if was happy or shocked but she promised to call Miss Buthelezi and ask her.

You could tell that my mom was bit worried about me but am a big girl I can take care of myself. I am ready to face my schoolmates and their taunts. As I left her room, she took her phone and texted Miss. I went to the kitchen to drink some water; I found my long-lost sister busy preparing dinner.

CHAPTER 2

" *S*ister*'s function as a safety net in a chaotic world simply being there for each other." - Carol Saline.*

Her name is Pretty, she's 2 years older than me. I asked what she was preparing, why was she preparing it and does she need any help. I ask questions a lot. Well, I helped her. For the first time was something I am doing with her willingly

We finished and I went to prepare the dining table while she came with plates and any other needed things. We both went to our rooms to prepare for dinner. My mom was still worried about me returning to school, she even tried calling my personal doctor she's a family doctor working at City Hospital.

Dr Nandi Ndlovu she's 27 years old, she's thick, light in complexion and have short hair. I call her by her first name or Nana that's how we used to call each other when I was at Psychiatric hospital. Well, she has no Kids or Man she lives alone, her family lives in the other province she visits only on holidays.

She wanted to ask if I was fit to go back to school but her phone kept going to voicemail. She then called Miss Buthelezi to ask for advice. I took a shower and went to my wardrobe to see what I can wear; I saw the dress my dad purchased for me on my birthday. It was pink with blue, white flowers.

I wore the dress with my black sunglasses and went downstairs to have dinner, while walking down the stairs my mom and sister looked at me. They complimented me a lot and my mom couldn't believe that the dress was still fitting me. Well, I was also surprised. While talking to my mom about the dress Pretty interrupted, I looked at her and my eyes were filled with fire. I hated her so much.

We had dinner, they were busy talking about how they were spending time together when I was gone. After few minutes I stood up. My mom asked what's wrong and we're having fun, I gave her a big fat reply.

"Well, you are having fun alone, I wasn't there when you two went to the mall, school camps and all. You know what good night this will also be a perfect time for you guys to create more memories without me disturbing you," I said.

I looked at Pretty and rolled my eyes ran upstairs. Went to my room and locked the door. As I left Pretty asked my mom why I hate her so much, what did she do wrong to deserve my hatred and my bad behavior, but my mom had no answers. She also stood up and left the dining room, went to her room, and threw herself on her bad and cried.

I sat on my bed and made a serious introspection. This one-sided tension of mine was starting to be a burden I don't even have a reason to hate her, I just hate her because she's my mom's daughter - that's madness, I mean if we become friends no harm will be caused that will make my mom happy. I looked at the time, wore my PJs and went to Pretty's room.

Knocked and went inside, I really don't know where to start, after Pretty came to stay with us I felt as if mom was giving her more attention than me and that made me jealous of her beside that I was the only child then boom I had to share my parents love with someone. I sat next to Pretty, held her hand and apologized she was so understanding, and she forgave me, pinching my cheeks with love, and she hugged me so tight.

For the first time I slept very peacefully after my dad left us. In the morning, I woke up, brushed my teeth, splashed water on my face and wiped it. I opened the curtains the sun was shining so bright, and the birds were singing, it was a very good day. I changed and went downstairs to have breakfast. Everyone was already having their food.

I told our mom about last night and how Pretty and I decided to spend the entire day together so that we can get to know each other better. My mom was so happy that she sang a happy song.

It was a GOOD MORNING INDEED.

After few hours Dr Nandi called my mom back. She apologized for missing her calls, told her how hectic it was for her last night. Had to do some surgery that it's why she couldn't get her. My Mom understood and asked her if I can go to school, Dr Nandi seen no problem with that, I was physically, mentally, and emotionally ready she said, and my mom understood.

In the evening my mom came to my room, I was in my blankets, ready to sleep. She got in and sat next to me.

"Hey sweetheart, how are you?" Said my mom.

"Oh, mom Hii, why aren't you asleep its late?" I said.

"No, I just wanted to know how you feel about tomorrow." She said.

My mom was really worried about me, but she did not have to worry because I am super excited, I really can't wait to meet all my friends. Well, she gave me a good night kiss on my forehead went to her room. I slept so well that I forgot to set an alarm but luckily Pretty woke me and we went to school together.

The first thing I did was to go to Ms. Buthelezi's class. I knocked and went inside. I faced down the entire time with shame, the last time I gave her attitude. I greeted her and she greeted back. Told her how sorry I was for the way I talked to her the last time. Really, I wasn't in a good space then, I was hurting and mourning. She stood-up came my way and held my hand and forgave me. She even gave me a tight hug.

My life was starting to be perfect. I became dedicated and made sure that I pass. Years passed on, Pretty and I passed our grade 12. We went to Varsity, became best friend but will our friendship last since we are in the new environment?

CHAPTER 3

*M*y first day at Varsity was a total mess with bit of excitement. I woke up very early and prepared for my class. I had no friend, nor did I know where the lectures halls are. I took my books and bag, went to the campus. While searching for the hall I bumped to this dark, tall, handsome guy. He was wearing a Jean with blue jersey and a hat with black shoes his name is Nick Jackson same age as me but second year student in different school.

I apologized, picking up my books on the floor and the guy helped me. Took the blame himself but I kept apologizing until he accepted it. When I was about to leave, he asked me something.

"Uhm before you leave, please help me, I am looking for this hall" he asked.

OMG the guy is looking for the same hall that I am looking for. I looked at him then laughed a bit, told him we are looking for the same Hall, he couldn't believe. I showed him my map. Is this what they call love at the first sight. We looked for the hall together till we find it and I felt so safe around the stranger.

The Varsity life was great but bit worried about my mom she was working on a very big project. That day she was getting ready for work, and she wore her long black dress, with black doek and blue hill. She went to Rosebank mall to meet with the client over breakfast and like I said my mom is smart she rocked the meeting and got the contract.

While I was still at the campus Pretty made her way there too but, on her way, she met this dark, tall, fine lady. But she was so weird, she had earrings everywhere, nose and lower lip. It was the first time they met but the girl already told how she likes Pretty; I mean that's very weird and too good to be true. Her name is Nkosazana Dlamini. Pretty thought it will be good to use her in her own advantage since she doesn't know around the campus and Nkosazana wants her number she had to earn them by showing her around. She had no problem.

There was influence, and rapidly. The parties and all but Nick oh Lord there's something attractive about him.

"It's our first day and they already giving us the assignment but that's good because I'll get to spend more time with Nick."

As everyone was leaving the hall Nick called out to me.

"Yes" I said.

Oh, when I turned my skirt lifted, he almost saw everything am given.

"Uhm, do you mind giving me your number so that we can help each other with this assignment?" He asked.

"OH no, not at all I really needed someone to study with since my sister and I do different courses," I said.

He gave me his phone and he looked so handsome. Surely God took his time to make him.

"There you go and please don't call me late at night," I said.

Smiled at him.

"Don't worry Shawty you'll get your beauty sleep," He said.

After reaching my room, I tossed myself on my bed and faced up, after some time I took my phone to check up on Pretty. Her phone kept ringing for some time but finally answered, there was weird noise in the background. It's like a club or something. She told me she's out with her new friend Nkosazana. I really had no problem with that at least she has a friend but was worried about the environment they are at.

Immediately after hanging up, phone rang, it was Nick I smiled a bit then came to my senses. I greeted and he greeted back. Silence took place for some time, I then asked how I can help him.

"I am about to go to library would you like to come with me?" Nick asked.

"Most defiantly, let me just change fast, I'll be there," I said.

"Actually, I am outside waiting for you," He said.

Oh, this guy, I looked through the window and he was there.

"Ok give me 5," I said.

I hang up and wore my track pants with running sneaker, took my phone and notebook and left. We drove from my flat to the library and no one said anything. Few hours later my mom called just to check up on us, but I couldn't be long because I was still in the library, and she couldn't reach Pretty's phone.

"Inhaled."

My mom is worried sick about Pretty and she's busy partying. After Nick dropped me at my place, I saw Pretty kissing Nkosazana, but I didn't know it was Nkosazana because we haven't met. And I could tell they were drunk; I came close to them and shout out Pretty loudly. They looked at me, scared when Pretty realized it was me she laughed.

"You nearly killed me." Pretty said.

I looked at them disgusted and pulled Pretty to our flat. I opened the door, pushed her inside and locked. Put my things on the table.

"Are you mad?" I said.

"Oh, please chill," Pretty answered.

I shouted at her harshly, but it was not helping. I wonder what's going on with her, haven't stayed even a week she started drinking.

(sighed)

I'll call mom and let her know. As I was about to get my phone it rang. Nick! What does he want currently. I answered the phone, didn't take me long I was smiling already at least I have someone who can cheer me up sometimes. I really wonder if he also feels what I feel when am around him. Conversation kept going till time wasn't on our side.

"Oh yeah just wanted to say good night," he said.

"This guy is too much, but I like it. At least I get good night what not."

"You are too much you should have just sent text," I said.

"Wanted to hear you voice," He said.

Am I blushing? No, I am in love or what's going on with me. He hangs up, I smiled, and I went to bed.

CHAPTER 4

"*The root of education is bitter, but the fruit is sweet." - Aristotle.* I woke up early today, got off the bed and went to bathroom to pee. shuuuuu what a relief. Got to get ready early today I have early class.

(sighed)

I went to the kitchen and had porridge while eating Pretty came.

"Hi little sister." Pretty said.

I looked at her and looked away.

"Hi." I replied.

"Are you good, how did you sleep?" She asked.

"Where were you last night?" I asked.

"Not that again please I got headache." she said.

"Alright." I said.

I got up from the chair and went to my room, took a quick bath, wore my black track suits with black Nike sneakers then went to the campus. Pretty is old I won't babysit her; I won't ask her anything anymore I'll just focus on my studies. Immediately when my eyes landed on the gate Nick was there with his red sport car, the beast. His car had gold rams too expensive. Is he stalking me or!

"Oh, hi Nick what are you doing here so early?" I asked.

"I thought we could go to class together," he said.

I looked at him and I was so annoyed. I do like him, but he is too much sometimes.

"That's so sweet of you but I don't like what you are doing, I feel as if you are stalking me. Don't you have life, don't you have any important things to do?" I asked.

"Wow that's harsh, sorry I'll see you at class." he said and turned.

"Eish I am sorry Nick; I didn't mean to, just that am worried about Pretty and I'll also appreciate if I also get to spend some time alone." I said.

(He laughed)

"You can tell me what's wrong? Ok I hear you I'll take a step back." He said.

I told him everything Pretty did last night and that she went out with is Nkosazana Girl. What's surprising is that he knows her and refuses to tell me about her. Is she a bed person! I just hope Pretty won't get into trouble because of her.

"Ok, can I get a lift." I asked.

He laughed at me, opened the door, and drove off. Reached and went to class. Few hours after I was in different hall and Nick kept cracking jokes couldn't handle myself, but I laughed almost the whole class. Message popped on my phone, I checked it, and it was from my mom saying.

"Matty why is Pretty's phone going to voicemail? Is she in kind of trouble or what. You better call me when you get a chance, or I'll drive all the way there and it won't be nice."

My face expression changed immediately, and Nick noticed asked me what's wrong and I told him it was my mom and read her message to him. He offered to look for Pretty with me after the class and I agreed. I became quite the whole time, couldn't listen anymore since my mind was elsewhere. The break time arrived Nick and I met Pretty near the gate waiting for Nkosazana, they're now dating. I asked to talk to her in private.

"When last did you speak to mom, she has been trying to call you, but your phone goes straight to voicemail. WHY and I hardly know you. You're always busy for me, you come back late sometimes drunk and worse of them all you don't return. What changed you sis talk to me?" I said.

She didn't even bother to answer me she kept rolling her big eyes. Meanwhile Nick was also busy talking to Nkosazana trying to talk sense into her but none of them was interested. They both left us there hanging but it's ok they know what they are doing. We went to library and Nick went to buy ice cream so that I can cheer up.

The first semester passed, Nick and I got our results, and we worked very well, unfortunately Pretty failed because she was a party animal, she had no time to study, and she hid it from our mom, and I couldn't say anything because it wasn't my place to.

Pretty had changed a lot and I became fad-up of her actions, I informed our mom and that caused chaos between Pretty and I. She started hating me, she even blacked my number and social accounts.

It was in the afternoon; I was busy studying and couldn't focus because of my situation with Pretty, my phone rang I looked at it and it was Nick. He sensed my mood. Just to cheer me up as always, he purchased two tickets to watch my favorite movie, I refused till I agreed he never gave up on me.

I hanged up got off the bed I was so excited, before taking a shower I looked for something I could wear. Uhm! I took out my short black silk dress with black hills. Wanted to look different, I always wear jeans and tracksuits. I then took a shower. After I have finished, I looked at the time then looked through the window to see if Nick has arrived or not, and he was there. I took my handbag, phone and went outside.

I greeted Nick and hugged him. He opened the car door for me, we both got in the car then left. While driving Nick complimented me, he told me how beautiful I was and how he can't get his eyes off me, nor can he concentrate on the driving.

This guy, I don't want to die, if he keeps staring at me, he'll bump into something.

But I was blushing like nobody's business.

We reached the Cinema got ourselves something to drink then went inside, sat next to each other and we had lots of fun. The place was amazing, we firstly watched "I'm in love with the church girl then fast and the furious 8". The gab that I had after my dad left was immediately filled.

CHAPTER 5

*I*t's not wrong for a girl to make the first move.

Later he drove me back, when we reached, we got off the car stared at each other for so long, none of us said anything my heart started racing my knees were shaking. I kissed him and held back a bit then kissed him again, he did not even stop me, but I guess it's a good thing.

I went to my room, had a long hot bubble bath, and wore my PJ's. I grabbed my phone sent Nick goodnight text and had my beauty sleep. Around 3 am message popped on my phone; it was from Nick.

"I can't sleep busy thinking about you. Where were you this whole time. Love Nick "

I sent message back.

"I was sleeping and dreaming about you, but you've disturbed my dream."

Only God can tell how madly in love I was! I went back to sleep. Few hours later Pretty woke up very drunk as usual. She fought with Nkosazana because she kissed some male friend of hers. While busy trying to get sober my mom called.

"Hello Ma," Pretty said.

"Oh, finally you answered my call," My mom said.

"Come on ma, am just busy with some stuff," said Pretty.

"Really, where are your results?!" Asked mom.

Oh Lord what is she going to do, she can't tell her that she failed.

"Uhm Ma, can I call you bit later am kind of busy right now." said Pretty.

She hangs up and sat straight. While thinking message popped in from my mom.

"I know you have failed Pretty you could have just told me. And I know you party every weekend I wonder what changed you. I am very disappointed with you. Your mom must be turning in her grave seeing you busy toying with your future like this. Anyway, just wanted to tell you am not feeling well it's been months now, you don't even visit just to check up on me. Please stop drinking and focus on your studies am not going to live forever."

Tears made their way on her face, she failed to be a good daughter. Wiped her tears and thought about what my mom said. WAIT!! How did she know she failed. Oh God it's obvious I am the one who told her. She got up ran herself a bath; after bathing she wore her white jean with white t-shirt and black sneakers, got her keys and went to see Nkosazana. On her way she met some old guy with his friends. They stopped their car Infront of her.

"Can we give you a lift." The guy asked.

"No thank you." She said.

Folded her arms and rolled her big eyes, like she always does. She tried playing hard to get but when she saw bottles of vodka, she saw her free tickets to heaven. She got inside the car, and they drove off, forgot about Nkosazana.

Many years past and finally Dr Nandi had boyfriend and they were staying together happily.

His name is Nkosinathi Jackson, 35 years old. He was running a family business and he's a qualified therapist. His family live in KZN here In Johannesburg it's him and his mom "Busisiwe" but everyone call her Mabusi and younger brother Mzwandile AKA Nick.

Him and Dr Nandi met at doctor's conference, they exchanged numbers, went on few dates then here they are. He's the best thing that has ever happened to her. His whole family loves her a lot and hers loves him as well. I forgot to mention they're engaged.

While I was still asleep message popped it was Nick wishing me a lovely day. The boy won my heart with his sweet words. Every single word that comes from his mouth was a fantasy. He painted my world with true love and friendship.

Well, I went to school and attended all my classes, but Nick was nowhere to be seen, he doesn't even answer my calls nor my texts. I started to think that he was ghosting me, or he was just playing with my feeling. Or kissing him was a bad idea or am I a bad kisser, but how can that be because we sent each other texts in midnight. Maybe he's busy, but at least he could have just sent me a text.

After all my tiring classes I went back to my room and took a nap. While sleeping my phone rang, it was Nick I was so mad that I ignored his calls. He called so many times and I never answered, it was not my intentions to fall for him.

He came to my room to check up on me. He knocked and I sent him back. Later around 9 pm I was busy doing my assignment my phone rang. It was Nick, this guy doesn't give up. I ignored his calls the whole day and he kept call after every 30 minutes. I decided to answer.

"What do you want". I asked.

"Is that the way to talk to your manfriend, What's wrong babe?" He asked.

"Nothing, why have you called," I asked.

"I was checking up on you, I called and came to your place, but you ignored me. why," He asked.

"Where were you today you did not attend classes, did not respond to my messages nor returned my calls?" I asked.

"Uhm, can we talk about this some other time? I really had a rough day." He said.

I asked him if he loved me, or if he was serious about me or wanted to waste my time. I am concern about my health because I only how I become if I lose someone I love. And he told me how much he loves me and how he wants to spend his entire life with me, I did not believe any word he said, and I hanged up.

My mom started getting sick even worse. Her brother went with her to different doctors, but nothing seems to help. She had brain tumor, how sad. They even tried traditional doctors; they lost all hope.

CHAPTER 6

" *T*he only way to get rid of a temptation is to yield to it. Resist it, and your soul grow sick with longing for the things it has forbidden to itself." - Oscar Wilde.

She started peeing and coughing blood. Her brother asked why she can't just tell me about her situation, but she says she doesn't want to stress her child.

They decided to go to a traditional doctor her friend recommended to her, Gogo Nolwabo that's her name. She's a very famous doctor and very powerful. My uncle and mom got into the car and drove off to see her. My Mom was the one driving and on their way her eyes because blurry Uncle Mfundo panicked that was his name.

They exchanged seats and drove off. Their journey was long they were going to a small village in Eastern Cape. They had 4 Stops already and my mom's vision was getting worse. So they stopped at some BnB for the night.

The following day was Saturday. I was doing my laundry and Nick showed up I was so annoyed seen him, he apologized, I tried playing hard to get until he shouted at me.

"Please will you stop being selfish and hear me out? (*Never seen this side if his it's shocking and he continued*) As I was saying my mom was in hospital she met with an accident, but it was nothing major she just broke her leg that is why I was not able to respond to your messages nor your calls," he said.

Tears made their way in his cheeks. I dropped the cloth I was holding and hugged him. I felt so bad after hearing the truth. I also apologized for being selfish. We hugged and he helped me clean here and there around the house.

Ever since Pretty shared room with her friends she always had problem with me, I try to stay out of her way but she the one who picks fight with me. The thing is that she wants Nick not because she likes him because I date him, her aim is to get back to me for telling our mom about the way she's behaving. Will this fight ever end?

Nick and I really had good time.

He was a great help indeed I was so tired after doing the laundry, had no energy for the dishes, cleaning and stuff. Plus, my man cooked for me, and I can say he's good at cooking. I got myself a real dude here.

"Baby, thank you for today," I said.

"It's all a pleasure my love and it helped us bond a bit you know." He said.

"Yeah, you're right. So how about the Assignment how far are you?" I asked.

"Am almost done, by tomorrow morning it will be done, you?" He said.

"Am also getting there but I'll need your help there and there." I said.

"OK. Uhm babe I think I should go. I promised my mom to come early today." He said.

He took the dishes to the zinc and drank some water.

"Alright sweetie, don't mind the dishes I'll do them." I said.

He laughed and turned at me.

"I wasn't doing them; I was drinking water." He said.

We laughed, he grabbed his keys, phone and gave me million kisses with hug on it. Nick opened the door, stepped outside and hugged me, Pretty arrived, she greeted and went inside.

My uncle and mom arrived at Gogo Nolwabo's place. They both went inside the creepy rondavel after sitting down Gogo said.

"You won't get your vision back; you will eventually go blind. This has nothing to do with ancestors its natural. (she's a straight talker she didn't want to waste any time) this is your way of leaving the world. You must be asking yourselves why am saying this. I don't only work for the ancestors; I can also communicate with God. I have so many gifts."

Tears made their way out. This was so heartbreaking, my mom didn't want to believe she started swearing at the Doctor, calling her names. I can understand she was hurt; she did not want to accept; she left the Rondavel and went to her car. My uncle apologized on her behalf, got up and they both made their way back home.

I hugged my man and he left, went inside sat down and looked at Pretty. She was very tired and stinking alcohol.

We argued, exchanged words and most of them were hurting but I acted normal because I am the one who informed my mom about her results, it's all my fault. While shouting at each other we heard a voice, looked at each other and faced the door.

"What the hell is going on here".

It was my mom and uncle. Her eyes were red like she was crying the whole night. They came our way.

"Mom when did you come, uncle why didn't you tell me you were coming?" I asked.

"I said what is going on here?" Asked my mom.

Her eyes were burning she was angry indeed, she was even shivering.

"Sis sit down, get water Matty." my uncle said.

She started coughing so bad, blood! what's happening.

"Mom! blood, Malume! mama...blood" I shouted.

"Malume what's happening to her? Mama, are you ok?" Asked Pretty.

"As if you care I pushed her, all of this is happening because of you Pretty, you're selfish. You...." I said.

My mom interrupted.

"Matty please".

Saying that holding her chest coughing badly, I rushed to sit next to her and held her hand.

"Mom what's wrong. Malume call an ambulance," I said.

Her eyes started looking weird and blood was coming from both her mouth and nose, she fainted. We went to the hospital. Everything was so blank.

Few hours later at the hospital, Nick came with his brother.

"Babe, babe how are you, is everything ok?" Nick asked.

I hugged him and cried so bad.

"I don't know," I replied.

I told them everything and his brother said he'll talk to Dr Nandi to help us little did I know he was talking about my Dr Nana that's what we used to call each other, we really leave in small world.

CHAPTER 7

" Where is something about losing a mother that is permanent and inexpressible - a wound that will never quite heal." - Susan Wiggs

After few minutes the nurse approached us.

"Nurse is my sister, ok?" My uncle asked.

"Unfortunately, I can't say right now but she has brain tumor," said the Nurse.

She left us there. I couldn't handle myself I cried out loud Nick tried to keep me calm but I couldn't handle myself after 30 minutes the Doctor came.

"Sorry we need to perform an operation please go to the reception and fill the forms." Said the doctor.

My uncle went to fill all that. Nick was hold me so tight and Pretty was standing there all alone. Everything is happening so fast. My mom was ok the next thing she has brain tumor; how did this happen? Oh Lord please be with her. After fill all forms my uncle tapped Pretty in the shoulder. She looked at him, hugged him and cried.

"Mshana, I know you Loved Ntobi like your mom, but we all visited this place one way or the other we all going to leave so please be strong," said my uncle.

"Uncle aunt treated me like her own daughter, I never lacked anything. She's the only person I have in this world God knows how much she means to me," said Pretty.

My uncle hugged her, and we were all crying.

[Inside the theater]

She was surrounded by doctors, still trying to help her. She couldn't breathe on her own, she had machines all over her. Then suddenly the machines beeped so fast, it was tense in that room.

"She is having a panic attack; her blood pressure is dropping." DOCTOR 1.

It was a very tense moment, her chest went up and down, they started running around, putting on drips and injecting her. the chest stopped moving.

Beeep… That's what they heard a long beep.

"We lost her." DOCTOR 2.

The doctor was remorseful.

"Time of death is 20:07." NURSE.

The nurse was filled with shame on her face as she said that. Nick and her brother tried making me drink water, but I just couldn't, I just wanted to see my mom, wanted to hug her, and kiss her but unfortunately it was too late.

"Bhuti is Sis Nandi in that ward to undated us," asked Nick.

"No, she said she had a workshop so she's not in," said Nkosinathi.

"Eish Matty please stop crying please you'll get sick," He wiped my tears.

"Matty my girl, sis look I know you love your mom so much, but she needs you strong and healthy so please stop crying for her sake," said Nkosinathi.

I nodded and wiped my tears. While waiting the doctor walked outside the theater and came to us. She took a deep breath. I already knew what she was going to say, I know that look I know it well.

"It's not what I'm thinking it is right doctor?" I said.

"We tried all we could, but unfortunately it was too late, we couldn't save her." Said the Doctor.

"No Malume she can't leave me like this Mama !!mama!!!" Said Pretty

"No Pretty don't cry it's going to be ok." said my uncle.

"But she… how, why so fast?" I asked.

I couldn't cry I was so hopeless.

"Babe, are you ok please say something," said Nick.

"I'm sorry my deepest condolences to you and your family." Said the doctor.

"No not my mother, you must be mistaken." I said.

"I'm sorry." Said the doctor.

She left us all heartbroken. I blamed Pretty for all this. I drove her out of my life. The funeral arrived and all the arrangements were good, I made sure my mom's funeral was the best. After the funeral everyone left, and I also left the house with one of my uncle's daughters. For the past few weeks everything was a crazy. But I started seeing therapist so that I can get my life back to line plus Nick's brother promised me a job as his assistant. And everything was easy with Nick by my side as for Pretty she started sleeping with older people for money because she was kicked out of school.

Nick and I went on the picnic, he proposed, and I agreed to marry him. We returned later, when I reached, I found Pretty sitting outside with all her bags. Nick and I were surprised.

I asked her what was wrong she told me that she was kicked out of her room with her friend because they have failed again, and the school did not fund them. I gave her place to stay for few days. It was the last semester schoolwork was hectic I had a lot on my plate, working and studying ah but it was for the best. At night we were having dinner with Pretty I told her about my engagement and about my financially problems

"Sister, I can't maintain you anymore," I said.

She looked at me.

"Really or is just because you want Nick to move in with you?" she asked.

"No, it's not like that, am not financially stable to feed the both of us," I said.

She just stood up took her phone and went out. She did not return that night, fine. The following day at campus I told Nick about what happened last night. After some time, I received a call informing asking me to be present with Pretty for my mom's will. I had a test to write in 30 minutes, I was already messed up did not even know how to inform Pretty because she doesn't even talk to me.

Nick offered to handle that one. I went to the hall to write, and Nick went to my room to inform Pretty. When he reached there, he found her drunk, he sat her down and told her. She behaved very weird, she started crying and hugging Nick, he tried pushing her away, but he was unable to. Pretty offered Nick a drink and he happily accepted it because he did not want, her to feel bad. They both got drunk, things got nasty Pretty slept with my Fiancé. This was one of her tricks to break Nick and I apart.

CHAPTER 8

" *It is easier to forgive an enemy than to forgive a friend." - William Blake.*

I got home after the hardest test of my life, worried about Pretty. When I reached, I opened the door. I could smell alcohol I went to my room, and I opened the door, my heartbeat so fast. I dropped my phone, Nick and Pretty noticed me. My Man friend betrayed me with my sister how cheap. I went straight to Pretty and choked her, Nick tried to stop me, and I kicked both out of my room. Nick shouted at Pretty.

"This is what you wanted right? You did this intentionally." Nick said.

"Oh, please stop acting like a child I know you also wanted me, Matty doesn't even give you sex at all. I know." said Pretty.

"It doesn't matter Pretty, I was willing to wait for her, I have changed am not the same Nick, who was a player last year like they say," he said.

Pretty and Nick were staying in the same neighborhood before she moved in with us. The hatred I've buried with difficulties came back. I wanted nothing to do with Nick. Like how he can sleep with my sister knowing that we still mourning for our mother? How heartless the world can be. I am from the family that is torn. The day for the WILL to be read arrived. My uncle and Pretty were already there when I arrived but they were still waiting for the lawyer. I got inside the house greeted my uncle and sat down. He noticed that I was not ok and not seeing the ring cleared his suspension.

"Mshana tell where your ring is?" He said.

"Uhm uncle I'll tell you later, not now please."

Pretty's eyes were looking here and there she thought I'll tell my uncle what she has done but no I won't not now. While drinking tea the lawyer arrived and apologized being late because of the traffic and we understood. She read us the rules first then the WILL and it stated that everything belongs to Me. She left nothing for Pretty and that made her mad at me.

I asked my uncle why my mom would do that and what he said to me was shocking. Pretty wasn't my mom's daughter; she was her sister's child she died after giving birth to Pretty. I didn't know what to say but I requested the lawyer to give some potion of my money to her, yes, I hated her, but she was still my sister. I brought myself a big house with 5-bedroom, kitchen, lounge,3 bathroom and 2 study room" and a black BMW car.

We parted ways and since from that day I never saw her and Nick's mom called me to her place to resolve the matter between us, we also parted ways but not for long. That day we decided to take our relationship to the next step, and I gave it to him fearing he'll get it elsewhere. Later he invited me to his place. I wore my long red dress with a doek and white sneakers. I got into my new white Ford car and went to him.

"The way I like things I make sure all the time that I get expensive things, I won that car at the auction last month."

I was so scared it was my first time and he made sure my first time was perfect. We had dinner then took things to the bedroom. The few months later things were still great between Nick and I; we were even expecting a child. One day I went to the mall to get few things for my unborn baby, and I met Pretty walking with her sugar daddy. I tried talking to her, but she pushed me, I fell and lost the baby. Now I had a reason to hate her. I wished her nothing but bad luck and everything in her life went as I wished.

Long time after the incident she came to my place and wanted to talk to me. I told her to never come to my place ever again asked her if she want to sleep with my man again. I blamed her of my mom's death and my child's. She was like whatever, I don't care I can get Nick if I want to.

The tension between us never ended and I really didn't care at all. Later Nick came back from work. I was busy cooking, and someone grabbed me from behind, and kissed my cheek. I closed my pots and turned into him I hugged him and greeted.

"How was your day?" I asked.

"Batter now that am home." Nick said.

He went to our room took off his clothes and took a quick bath since the dinner was ready. I came into the room took out his blue pjs and tossed them into the bed and went downstairs to set the table. He came we ate, and I told him about Pretty, he cleared his throat, I looked at. Like why he is doing that after I mentioned Pretty's name.

"What's wrong." I asked.

"Uhm, I met her few days ago and I gave her money." he said with shame.

"You what? You can't be serious." I said.

I was so hurt why will he hide such a thing to me, are they Still seeing each other. I took a pillow got him out of my bed. And pushed him outside the room.

"I don't share room with cheaters." I said.

I locked myself. He slept on the guest room, the next morning he found me in the kitchen already having my breakfast. He asked for his and I gave her a big fat reply, with disrespect.

"Since you can keep things from me, I guess you can also make some for yourself," I said

And I left him standing there.

Took my back, keys and left. While driving I met Nkosazana on the roadside, I greeted her, and she recognized me immediately and she told me about Pretty's condition. I was so sad couldn't believe I shouted at Nick without hearing him out, whereby he was helping my sister to get meds. I got to my workplace, and I couldn't. concentrate, should I call him I sent him message apologizing but he blue ticked me.

I stoop-up and went to close the door, as I was closing it someone pushed it from outside. I looked and it was Nick.

CHAPTER 9

" *A girl should be like a butterfly. Pretty to see, hard to catch." - Coco Chanel.*

I went to sit down, and he closed it, I kept apologizing, but he didn't even want to listen. I stood up and went to hug him and he lovely opened for me. We kissed and kissed and kissed, he went to lock the door and made me sit on top of the table.

"I am the man of this relationship." he said.

Busy taking off my panty.

"I know." I said.

He pulled me closer and kissed me on the neck.

"You don't get to talk to me as you please. I'll show you who is the man." he said.

"Baby am sorry." I said.

He kept kissing me went down on his knees, his tongue played its magic down there after few minutes he took me to the couch, opened my thighs and put it all inside. I moaned loudly but no one could hear me. He sexed me slowly and slowly till I whispered.

"Baby faster."

After that we dressed up and I apologized once more and told him that Nkosazana told me everything. He forgave me, kissed my forehead, left and I carried on with my work.

Pretty's health condition started getting worse, she was even addicted to drugs. She had only herself, I tried helping her, but she didn't want anything to do with me. But as time goes by, she came to me for help. It was on Friday in the afternoon, and it was raining heavily.

Nick was watching a movie, and I was preparing supper, his family was supposed to join us, but his mom was too busy with her work only his brother and Dr Nandi were able to come. I finished my chores, made my way to the bedroom to get ready.

While I was busy getting dressed doorbell rang could not see or hear who it was but assumed it was Nick's brother and his woman. After getting ready I went downstairs on my way down my eyes met Petty. I wanted to turn back but I thought it would be unfair to not hear her out. I greeted her and sat beside Nick. Offered her something to drink.

My sister wasn't herself; she wore torn shoes and clothes. I asked her if she'll like to join us for dinner and she happily agreed. I went upstairs with her, ran her a bath and gave her something to wear. In few hours Nick's brothers sent a text apologizing for not being able to make it because of some stuff. I dished up and we had our food. After wards she wanted to leave but we asked her to stay for the night and she agreed. After all this tiring day I was getting in bed, and Nick was waiting for me.

"Can we talk." He said.

"Ok." "Matty, do you think its ok for Pretty to stay for the night?" he asked.

I looked at him and couldn't believe what am hearing, didn't want to continue with this conversation, so I just switched off the lamb on my side and slept. In the morning, I got up early, had to prepare Nick's suit he has an important meeting. I ironed his clothes then went to the guest room to check on Pretty and she was not there, not to mention Nick's laptop was missing. I went back to my room to wake Nick up and prepared breakfast for him. After having his food, he went back to take his files and laptop bag.

"Baby, haven't you seen my laptop, I left it here last night." He said.

"Where?" I asked. "On the charger, wait where's Pretty?" he asked.

"Uhm, I don't know really, when I went to check up on her she was already gone." I said.

"You see that's what I was trying to talk to you about last night, but you never listen, I hope you're happy now!"

He left; he was mad. How can I be so careless? I wonder what will happen to Nick now, his presentation was saved there. I called his brother told him everything and begged for his help, he told me not worry he'll handle it. Just wanted to find Pretty and slap her hard and surely, she has sold it for money so that she can buy some drugs. I went upstairs and changed, grabbed my keys and handbag. I drove around the streets hoping to find her but no luck, on the other hand Nick isn't responding to my messages. After 2 hours I got a call from police station, I went straight there. I found Pretty drunk with her friends.

"Is she your sister?" asked the Policewoman.

"Yes, she is, what did she do?" I asked.

"They stole laptops, phones and we found drugs with them."

The lady said. I couldn't believe it; I didn't even bother to bail her out maybe if she spends a night she'll come to her senses. I asked the lady if I can look at the laptops hoping to find Nick's and I did. I got into my car and took a deep breath, drove to Nicks office praying that the meeting hasn't began. When I reached there, I asked the receptionist if he is in the meeting or not, but I was 10 minutes late. I gave her the laptop to give it to him if possible and left note on it. I had an assignment to submit to I passed by to school, dropped it and went straight home. I was still studying and had a job on the side.

After I have reached, I sat few minutes inside the car and send Nick's brother message saying am not feeling well, so I won't be able to make it to work today. I went inside the house and tossed myself on the couch. I don't think I'll ever trust Pretty ever again.

Nick's meeting went great than I expected. He brother kept his word, after going to his office the receptionist followed him and gave him the laptop, he thanked her and closed the door, listened to all my voice messages and texts but did not respond.

CHAPTER 10

" *Trust is not simply a matter of truthfulness, or even constancy. It is also a matter of amity and goodwill. We trust those who have our best interests at heart."* - Dean Koontz.

Usually after his meetings he comes to my place but today things were different, I made dinner hoping he will show up but no, I waited till I decided to go to bed. Before then I called his mom asking for him and he was not there also. Later his brother sent me a text informing me not to worry he's with Nick, I guess his mom told them I was asking about his whereabouts.

I haven't spoken to Nick for 3 days now and today I did not feel like going to school but I had no choice. I forced myself out of the bed and took a quick shower wore my jean and blue top and sport shoes. I was hoping to meet him at school, but he did not come, I guess he had something Important to attend to.

Later I went to Police station to bail Pretty but I was too late, my uncle already bailed her out. I went to Nick's place after leaving police station to check up on him, and I found his mom's car on the driveway.

"Is he ok?

She never visits him unless it's an emergency. I got of the car took my handbag and phone.

" I knocked and his mom opened for me, she was super happy to see me. I got inside, found his and Dr Nandi's uncle's busy discussing the date of Nkosinathi and Dr Nandi's wedding. I went upstairs with his mom. Dr Nandi was inside the room, nervously, going up and down. I sat her down, gave her water and waited for her aunt to come and call us. While waiting we heard ululation. We stood up and danced, Nick's mom gave me some dress to wear before taking the bride downstairs.

Everything went well, Nick was so busy for me. After few hours everyone was leaving. I walked his mom to her car, waved till they disappeared. Went back into the house found Nick going upstairs.

"Can we talk?" I asked.

He turned and made his way down. Sat down and I sat on the other couch.

"Baby I am sorry for not listening to you, Nick please forgive me, but I had no choice she's, my sister."

"Yeah, I hear you, and I also want to apologies for being too hard, just that you can't trust Pretty, and you know it."

We buried the hatch between us. We never get mad on each other for long but this time I really broke his heart. Time went to fast the wedding day has finally arrived, I was the maid of honor, and my man was the best man, everything was perfect. The Dr and her Husband had the wedding every girl could dream of.

The following day there was too much work to do, taking off the decoration and all, but I managed all since the new weds went on their honeymoon and Nick was caught up with some work. Later I was about to take a nap, the doorbell rang, I went to open. It was my uncle and Pretty, I was so happy to see him after so long, I gave him a warm hug, offered them something to drink.

Pretty wasn't well at all, she was very skinny and coughing very badly, I gave her water and she asked to sleep a bit. I was worried that she'll steal something again, so I just let her sleep on the guest room downstairs. I sat with my uncle and had a long chat before he could tell me what brings him here.

"Matty surely you can see Pretty is not well." He said.

"Yes, uncle what is the matter actually?" I said

I only knew Pretty was sick, but I did not know what the actual problem was, I was shuttered to know that my sister is suffering from HIV, and she cannot afford her treatment, my uncle also tried helping but he could not anymore, he just lost his job.

Tears made their way out; I got up went to the room Pretty was sleeping. I sat beside her, brushed her hair with my hand, crying. I failed to notice that my sister is suffering. Even though she can be stubborn sometimes, she does not deserve this. I went back to the lounge; Nick was already home.

Seeing my eyes red he got worried and asked my uncle what happened. He told him everything, got up from where he was, came my way, hugged me, and told me everything is going to be ok. I nodded and asked my uncle if he's going to stay for dinner, but no he had to leave, he had a long way to go. I asked him to leave Pretty behind, I wanted to take care of her myself. With Nick by my side everything was easy. Pretty started her treatment as soon as possible, I even added her on my medical aids should anything happen.

In few days it was my birthday. Before I left for my class Nick and Pretty were already preparing for it, I thought it was just a dinner but no. I came back from school and Nkosinathi's car was on the driveway it was a blue KIV with dark windows.

When I was about to get out of the car Nick's mom got it and asked me to drive her to her place, I was tired, but did it. When we reached there, she asked me to get in. She was acting all weird, offered me something to drink and asked me if I'll like to take a nap, I was shocked, but happily agreed, needed it after all. After few hours she woke me up and I took a long hot shower, when I got off the shower I found a dress on the bed, called Mrs. Jackson asked her what's going on, she just kept laughing at me and she was also ready, she looked stunning.

CHAPTER 11

"*The great thing about getting older is that you don't lose all the other ages you've been." - Madeleine L 'Engle.*

She was wearing a black dress with diamonds, with black hills and pure diamond necklace and her afro hair. I just dressed up quickly, she got me same dress as Her's but with different color, mine was dark blue and dark blue hills. And pure diamond necklace also, I felt like a Queen I am, I really felt honored. After getting ready I went downstairs, and we left. We stopped to some restaurant on our way, drank something and went back to my place around the corner she blindfolded me. I knew already what was going on, did not want to show her, how happy I was. The last time I celebrated my birthday it was when I was 6 years old.

We reached, helped me walk inside the house, after closing the door she took out the blindfolder I heard *HAPPY BIRTHDAY* song, all my friends were there, my colleagues and family, I even sheared a tear. Nick came to me with a wine, hugged me and wished me a happy birthday. We had fun but wish my mom was still around to enjoy this moment with me. Later everyone left and I had to clean up the mess. Well Nick helped me, and we slept early, after a very long day.

The following day I had to take Pretty to see the doctor, also had to go shopping. We got ready and I just wore sports "Blue top, black trackpads and white Nike sneakers." Got inside the car and waited for Pretty, I did not wait long, she came out and we hit the road. We reached the hospital and Dr Ndlovu was already expecting us, she ran few tests, and subscribed her to her meds. We left and she asked me to leave her around the corner, my heart was against it, think she will meet her old friends and get back to her old ways. I did as she asked, left, and hide somewhere so that I can see what she is up to. Just as I thought she was on up to something.

Some red GTI stopped, and she got inside. This one will never learn she was with the very same old man I saw her with at the mall, the day she pushed me.

(Inhaled)

I got in my car and left. *"How can Pretty be so careless, she's thinks drinking will help her get rid of her sorrows, argh she's old she knows what's best for her."*

I packed and went inside the mall, walked around looking for some dresses while looking my eyes landed at so Olive-green short dress, I immediately took it and looked for a handbag and shoes that matches it. *"Tip ladies always make sure your handbag is the same color as your shoes".*

I took out my bank card and paid. Took my bags to the car and drove off, on my way I passed MacDonald I am their regular customer plus I know how much Nick love their burgers. By the way I was on my way to his office to surprise him with lunch, he works very hard, he sometimes does not eat.

"Hello Charlie, how are you?" I said.

"Hey Matty, am good you?" the waiter said.

"I am good, please give me the usual" I said.

He smiled at me and left, while waiting for my order. My high school friend came Gift Ngwenya. I could not believe it. She was mother if 3, married and run her own business. In few minutes my older came, you never wait for long. Great service. Gift and I exchanged numbers to set a date to have lunch together, for old time's sake.

I left and in 45 minutes I arrived took out the food and walked in. All eyes were on me, some were giving me fake smiles, but I cared less. I asked the receptionist if Nick was busy, but no his schedule was clear, I went to office, and he was on phone. I walked in and unpacked silently without disturbing him.

While waiting he finally hang up, looked at me and gave me a smile. He got up and sat beside me.

"What can I be without you." He said.

I smiled wish I could spend more time with him, but he got lot of work to do. We ate, fed each other. As time was flying fast, I had to go because he must continue with his work. He went back to his desk, and I cleaned up, kissed him on a cheek and left.

On my way to the parking load, I met his mom, she had tiffin on her hand, I giggled hugged her and gave each other kisses.

"How are you, my child?"

"I am good mama you?"

"I am good too baby."

"Are you here to see Nick?"

"Oh yeah, I came to have lunch with him."

I could not hold myself I laughed told her we just ate.

She gave me that *"You're the one for my son/ What could he be without you"*. Look.

She still went to see him; she misses her sons also invited her for dinner. She is lonely these days. I left, after parking Pretty came greeted and went inside the house. I sat on the car for few minutes just wanted to clear my head before preparing for dinner. I got off the car went inside and Pretty was doing the dishes. I told her I have guests and she was happy to help me prepare for dinner. We started cooking and I decided to prepare Mabusi's favorite. She like tripe and papa, with few salads aside.

I forgot to get a wine; her mom likes it a lot. I texted Nick asked him to come with it for me and he agreed. Round 6 pm he knocked out, made his way to mall to get what I've asked. As he arrived his brother's car was on a driveway, he brought a new car, grey GTI with sliver rams, classic. He got in, and he was so happy to see Nkosinathi. Went upstairs to change, I've already chosen him something to wear. I also made my way in our room; Dr Nandi was helping me with preparing the dining table. Nick was taking a bath; I took off my clothes and joined him.

CHAPTER 12

"*H*appiness in marriage is not something that just happens. a good marriage must be created. In the art of marriage, the little things are the big things." - *Willard f. Harley Jr.*

He was so tired, he was just standing there with tap on, I got in rubbed his shoulders, down to his waist, he turned and kissed me. We kissed, kissed, and kissed we felt heat and made it fast.

We got dressed quickly, everyone was waiting for us. I was wearing a blue dress, and my man was wearing his black shirt with black chino and snakeskin shoe, brown on. We then went downstairs.

"All eyes on us"

We sat down had a chat and our newlywed told us about their honeymoon. Speaking of newlyweds Mabusi asked when we are getting married, we have been engaged for 7 months now, and it has been a very long journey.

"Already it feels as if we are married. He never let me lack anything, he is caring and loving, Nick really husbands me the way I want to be husband."

Well, we decided to get married the next month, but I was thinking it's too soon. I wish to graduate first. Later, everyone left, Pretty went to her room after cleaning the table. Nick and I did the dishes. I finished and went to bed. I was so tired that I immediately fell asleep after getting in sheets. Around 12 am I woke up, had pain, feeling dizzy and felt like vomiting. I got up the bed and went to the toilet, I sat beside the toilet seat for a while after vomiting my lungs out. Nick knocked and got inside.

"Baby what's wrong?" He asked.

"I really don't know my love, I...." I said.

Vomiting, and my stomach hurt a lot.

Nick went back into the bedroom and called Dr Nandi and she did not waste time; in a blink of an eye, she was here. They helped me sit on the bed, ran some tests.

"I really don't know if I should be happy or not, it's still early. I AM PREGNANT"

Nick was so happy; he was all over the moon, he kept kissing me. As I laid in bed and Nick walked Dr Nandi out. He came back and I was fast asleep, he got me inside the sheets, kept rubbing my tummy until only God knows.

The following day I woke up and Nick was not in bed, I was about to go to the bathroom, Nick came in.

"No, where are you going?" He asked.

"To the toilet." I said.

I looked at him, he was acting strange, yeah, he is caring and all, but he was too much. He helped me get up, I peed, and he was standing there waiting for me. Already after all that he gave me breakfast and made sure I finish it all. Took a bath and went back to sheets, my husbands to have ordered me to stay home today and I did exactly that.

Around 11 am I went downstairs, I was hungry so went to make something to eat. Pretty was standing near the zinc busy giggling with her phone.

"Hy Matty, how are you feeling now? Nick told me not to disturb you because you're not ok." She said.

"Hy big sis, yeah I am ok now, just feeling hungry that's all." I said.

"Should I make something for you?" she asked.

"Yes please, a toast with cheese will be fine and some orange juice." I said.

She made them while having the conversation going until it was the time, I wanted to share the pregnancy news with her.

"Uhm Pretty I want to tell you something." I said.

"Cleaning a throat."

She kept doing food for me while listening.

"I am pregnant." I said.

I know I dropped a bomb, but was not expecting that reaction, she just took her phone and left without saying a word nor without giving me my food. I stood up and finished what she started and went upstairs. After eating I bath, wore other PJs, slippers and went to prepare dinner. While in the kitchen Nick came in, gave me a kiss, and rubbed my tummy, he made me sit down and carried on preparing dinner. Talked about his day and mine. As we were busy talking, I told him about what Pretty did early, he just shook his head.

Thoughts started running through my mind, is she not happy for me or does she still want Nick.

I couldn't even share my thoughts with Nick, but my mind never rested. When he was done cooking, we both went upstairs, he took a shower, wore pjs too. We had dinner and our early night; he had meetings tomorrow. We got inside sheets I faced the other way, Nick came closer, squeezed my breasts while kissing my neck. I started breathing heavily.

Usually, we never have sex if one of us has meeting tomorrow, I don't know why but I made it culture.

He knew he got me where I wanted as I started breathing more heavily, most pregnant women never say no to sex because of the pregnancy.

In the morning Nick woke up early and his mom was already on my doorsteps. She was asked to take care of me as if I am sick. Little did he know I was about to be taken shopping. Around 9:30 Mabusi woke me up and I took a quick shower, wore my black tracksuits and grey sneakers.

Went downstairs, breakfast was ready waiting for me. We ate and had a long chat. I wasn't even aware that Pretty did not return yesterday, surely where ever she is, she's drunk worse she must be in some old man's bed.

Well, after our long gossip I took my car keys, handbag, and phone heading to the door.

"What are you doing? You are never driving when I am around." She said.

The lady spoke and I had to obey her. We laughed, just took my handbag and phone. We got in the car; she made sure I don't forget to put on the seatbelt. We drove off the car and reached the mall, as we got off the car the smell from hungry lion store made me crave for their wings. I told Mabusi I feel like having them. We went in, ordered while waiting for the order we had something to drink. Suddenly I got sick, our day was ruined already.

CHAPTER 13

"*A good husband makes a good wife." - John Florio.*
After five minutes reaching Nick's place he knocked, his mom can't keep secrets, so I nicely asked her not to tell him. He came with Dr Nandi poor lady can't work in peace.

She ran few tests and told us we'll get results in two days. Nick was extremely mad at his mom. But calmed down in few minutes.

"Baby it was not her fault, I was craving for Hot wings." I said.

"Fine but please next time if you need something just tell me, I'll get it for you."

"OK so do you know I got important meeting tomorrow."

He turned my way and I looked away. As always when I look away it means I am done talking and Nick knows that too. His mom left; he ordered pizza none of us had energy to cook. While waiting for the pizza, he washed my feet and massaged them, only I know him. It was one of his tricks to get Me to talk about the meeting I have tomorrow.

After my massage session we watched the big bang theory,

"*My best scene is when they said Sheldon should not say a word while doing as research. With some engineer from the army. Doing some invention*"

After few minutes someone knocked, I went to open, Nick was on a phone call. Our pizza arrived. I took out plates, and poured drink, he can't drink wine if I can't. We're on this pregnancy together. Its treatment me better than the first one, no morning sickness but lot of cravings and gained weight a bit and lot of mood swing.

Finally, daddy to be hang up. He sat next to me, fed each other. I don't remember the last time Nick and I spent a quality time. We just ate and I was feeling sleepy already, the kid is full, so we must sleep. The way I was so tired I just wore my PJs without taking a bath. I got in sheets and in 5 minutes I was asleep like a baby.

Early in the morning my phone rang, it was Pretty. She spent 2 days wherever, without informing me and I did not care. She was outside the house but unfortunately, I was at Nick's, and I never gave her a key because I don't trust her. After what she did, stealing Nick's laptop, I lost all faith in her. I asked her to come back later. I woke Nick thought he was going to work but no.

I went to the rest room. Then took a quick shower and prepared breakfast, it's been a while since my man ate food prepared by me. Made him breakfast in bed, nothing too much but classy, eggs, bacon, hashbrowns, toast and coffee just the way he likes it, strong black, Jacob coffee.

I woke him up, he was so happy. Smiled at me and kept blowing kisses. While eating I was getting ready.

"Where are you going?" He asked.

"My place." I said.

"Why?" He asked.

"A friend of mine is coming by; we were supposed to meet at the mall but because of my suddenly sickness I can't risk going out." I said.

"A friend." He said.

"Yeah, a friend her name is Gift Ngwenya we were on the same class from grade 8 to 11." I said.

He took a deep breath, he was not convinced, surely, he thinks am lying. But I am not. I finished getting ready, asked him to drive me to my place and he did. Quickly as we reached, he took a shower, helped me with food since he does not believe so I asked Gift to come with her partner. Our guests were supposed to be here by 12 but they are 30 minutes late, I guess they are stacked in traffic.

Not long after I sat down the doorbell rang; Nick opened the door. Gift was looking so beautiful; she was wearing blue formal dress with its top and black shoes. They were matching with her husband, but he was wearing brown shoes. We gave them a warm welcome. They sat down offered them something to drink. We had a chat before dishing up, it was great having them. I guess we'll visit each other more often plus Nick and Mr. Ngwenya really get along they were even planning to start a business together.

"REALLY NICE."

Gift helped me dishing up, while we were eating Pretty entered, drunk.

"Uhm this is my sister Pretty, Gift surely you still remember her." I said.

Stood up, faced down with shame. Nick cleared his throat, and I gave him that scary look.

"Oh yeah how can I forget her, Hi Pretty." Gift said.

"Oh hi." Said Pretty.

She went straight to her room. I've being so ashamed especially in my own house.

"So, Mr. Ngwenya how's business, must be tough. Meeting after meeting." Said Nick.

Trying to change the subject, my sweet babe. He can see I am not comfortable talking about this.

"Since when Pretty drinks?" Asked Gift.

I looked at Nick then faced my plate. Had no idea how to answer that.

"Uhm Since she joined Varsity. She has Changed a lot, but we'll talk about that sometime." I said.

"Sure." Said Gift.

We had our meal and later our guests left, promised to visit again. As we got back inside, I tossed myself on a couch, placed my feet on the table and took a deep breath. Nick was doing the dishes and cleaning up the table.

"I really had enough of Pretty, it's time for her to find her own place, I just can't take this anymore. Can't even talk to Nick about this, not in the mood for I told you so."

"Baby you'll find me upstairs am tired and please bring water for me." I said.

"Ok baby."

Stood up and made my way to my room. I sat down on the floor, it felt so great, these pregnancy makes me do unusual things. After few minutes I took my phone Scrolled through my contacts, wanted someone to talk to, someone who won't judge me or my decisions. I finally made up my mind and called my uncle. His phone kept ringing and ringing. Threw the phone in on the bed, took the pillow and slept on the floor, it felt comfortable after all.

CHAPTER 14

M*abusi is always lonely, she only has her sons who are always busy for her. Mr. Jackson died 3 months after Nick's birth, he had TB and refused treatment. Mabusi drowns herself with work and one thing I like about her is that she never forgets shopping."*

She was In Durban for a meeting, but few hours before she was in the mall, strolling, feeding her eyes. Some guy bumped into her, same age but still looking fresh. He was well built, no mustache, had chest, tall and dark. His name was Jack Zweli. They went to the Same school but never talked.

"Hi, are you Busi?" He asked.

Shaking hands.

"Oh, hi yes, Jack, right?". She said.

"Thought you forgot me." He said.

"No-no, how can I forget our school RSCL president." She said.

They laughed.

"I wish time was on our side but have to rush, I have a meeting in 10 minutes." She said.

"Oh alright, I also have to be somewhere, it was nice seeing you." He said.

They went different ways little did they know they are attending the same meeting, Mabusi after packing her car Jack called out to her, they were shocked to see each other there but they cleared it up. They both went to the meeting, and it took almost 3 hours, they then decided to grab dinner together so that they can catch up.

They went to some Indians store to try Pakistan food; it was chilly but delicious. After that Mabusi went back to her hotel to rest, she still has a long day tomorrow. Nit forgetting, they exchanged numbers.

After doing the dishes Nick watched soccer, Pirates was playing with Cape town city and CTC won the match. When he got into the room, he was scared seeing me on the floor, probably he thought I fell off the bed or fainted. He woke me up.

"Oh baby, what time is it? I've being waiting for you."

"Are you mad, do you want to get sick?"

He was mad, to avoid fighting I just apologized. He helped me sit on the bed and ran a hot bath for me. My baby was sad, he won't even look me in the eye, but he'll be fine. I took a bath and wore warm PJs and went to sleep. In midnight I woke Nick up.

"Baby I am hungry."

Without any fighting he just stood up and went to the kitchen to make me food, while busy there Pretty came to drink water.

"Hi Nick. "She said.

"Hy Pretty." He said.

His mind was elsewhere and Pretty on the other hand wanted to say something.

"Say it, there is no need to keep staring at me." He said.

"So really you are going to be a father and someone's husband soon?". She asked.

Nick was shocked, clearly, he did not see that one coming.

"Yes, I am happy, why?" He said.

"What about the Chemistry between us, you can't tell me you don't feel that when am around." She said.

"Wait what Pretty, you can't be serious. Your sister is carrying my baby, and we are soon to get married above all that I love her and respect her, whatever that has happened between us it was a mistake, and it was long time ago. Move on." He said.

"Oh really, but you know she doesn't give it to you like I did." She said.

Coming closer and trying to seduce him.

"Pretty please all that energy you're using to seduce me you should use it to take your treatment and for God's sake you're HIV positive, focus on your health." He said.

He left her there and came back to our room. What Nick said to her kept playing in her mind and that made her really mad she even broke a glass by just squeezing it. I ate my food as my tummy was hurting Nick rubbed it till, I fell asleep.

"The following day…"

Mabusi nearly woke up late but luckily Jack woke her up, they had another meeting, so he wanted to go together with her. She woke had a quick bath, wore a black with orange lines full dress with black hill, and black handbag. They went to the meeting but driving Jaks's car, black IPolo vivo.

They had all day meeting with 5 minutes break between. In the second break she called me.

"Hello Ma, how are you?" I said.

"Hello baby, I am tired shame, how is my grandchild doing." She said.

"Great, just missing Grandma that's all." I said.

We laughed; she doesn't want to be called that. She hangs up and went back to her meeting. Around 6 pm they finished and that was their last meeting. Since she was leaving tomorrow Jack asked her to have dinner with her, it might be their last time meeting who knows. Mabusi totally agreed.

Went back to her hotel room to freshen up. They met at the famous restaurant in Durban.

"You look beautiful." Jack said.

"Thank you and you also don't look bad." She said.

They laughed and had their meal. While eating some jazz bend was performing.

"This one is for our new couples in this restaurant." Said one of the singers.

They looked at each other and their eyes locked.

"Can you please dance with me?" He said.

She looked around, yeah, she's talkative but shy.

"Ok sure." She said.

They went to the dance floor; Jack held her by her waist and pulled her close she even closed her eyes. While dancing.

"Uhm how come you're still single with all this beauty." He asked.

"I am a widow, mother of 2 son's don't mean to break but successful sons." She said.

She said that proudly with confidence.

"Oh, sorry I did not know, so after your husband?" He said.

"I've never being with another man." She said.

"Really, but why." He said.

"I had to raise My kids besides I haven't met the perfect match." She said.

"Oh, ok I hear you, but I think you have found one now." He said.

Mabusi did not have words. They danced till the song finished. Everyone clapped and they went back to their table.

CHAPTER 15

" *It is never too late to love again because love is natural. It comes when you let your guard down. Love is precious."* - Rita Mae Brown.

Later Jack drove Mabusi back to her hotel, he asked for room number using the excuse that he wants to pop by tomorrow morning before leaving and Mabusi gave it to him.

Back at her room she kept smiling all along, took off her clothes, as she was about to get in the shower someone knocked. Bang it was Jack, as she opened the door he kissed her, closed the door with his leg. Mabusi stepped back at bit, Jack came closer.

"I don't know what it is but what am feeling for you is very strong." he said.

Mabusi kissed him, they felt hit things got nasty.

As for me, my life was not exciting as Mabusi's. I am 5 months pregnant now, we even postponed the wedding till the baby arrives, as per my wish I'll graduate before getting married. Nice!

Nick took me out for dinner tonight, after so long he Finally made peace with the fact that he can't keep me at home forever. I also need to see people, need to shop. I own myself a new wardrobe after this pregnancy.

As always Hungry Lions' Wings, that's what keeps me going. But I am not allowed to eat lot of them, I love outside meals, but they make me sick. We ate and drove back hope. As he stopped on the driveway, I was horny and I could see he is too, I kissed him while rubbing his dick, when it was hard, I stopped kissing him, I sucked him, he squeezed my arm painfully, but I kept going, he cammed in my mouth and I swallowed. While fixing ourselves.

"Wow baby what was that." He said.

"Starter you'll get desert later." I said.

"Oh ok." He said.

He took out grocery's plastic out, helped him with the light ones. We got inside the house, Pretty was playing Nick's PlayStation, she knows he does not like when his things are used without his permission but there, we go my trouble sister does not like peace.

As we enter Nick's face expression changed immediately. He just banged thing on the table and ran upstairs. I Knew exactly why so had to fix my mess.

"But Pretty why?" I said.

"Why what?" She said.

"You Nick don't like people using his things without his permission. "I said.

"It's just a TV game, what's the big deal."

Her attitude annoyed me, I went sat down near her.

"The big deal is, you don't contribute anything here, you just eat, sleep, bath and leave worse use our things without our permission and give us attitude. "

She stopped playing and I continued.

"I just can't anymore Pretty, I tried but I can't. I pay your medical bills, but you don't appreciate me, at least look for a job, do something with your life." I said.

"I am not physically fit to work and besides it's hard to get a job these days, so I can't work." She said.

"You can't or you won't. "I said.

"Both." She said.

"Alright. But you'll have to find your own place, you're becoming a burden now. I am giving you two days, after that I want you gone." I said.

I was so serious, she took her jacket, left, and banged my door. I couldn't careless, just stood up and took groceries out, then went to my room. Nick on the bed facing the ceiling, I sat next to him and faced up too.

"Are you ok?" I asked.

"Yeah." He said.

I know my man something is eating him.

"Baby I am sorry for Pretty's behavior. I've talked to her, promise it won't happen again. "I said.

"Yeah sure." He said.

"Come on Nick talk to me." I said.

I really don't have patience; I know my sister is wrong, but I can't keep apologizing. He took a deep breath.

"What can I say, all I know is that Pretty is doing this deliberately." he said.

"What do you mean?" I asked.

"Are you hungry? No, you must be." He said.

He simply ignored my question, went downstairs to prepare something for me. I know I am always hungry but not this time. My brain worked overtime trying to fix his puzzle. When he got back, I was already in sheets. I just covered my head and looked the other side.

"No baby you must feed my child." He said.

"I will only feed your child if you tell me what you meant." I said.

"Later at least, for now eat." He said.

I stood up, too a pillow and blanket from the cupboard and placed them on a couch.

"You'll sleep there, until you decide to tell me the truth. "I said.

I got into sheets and switched off the lights. Electricity is expensive so he'll use his phone for light. I was mad, we promised not to keep secrets from each other anymore, but Nick never stayed in his promises.

"Oh, Matty please, you can't be serious. Or is this the way you want me to leave your place, you know I can't sleep on a couch, and you never let me sleep on guests' rooms." He said.

He should not have said I want him to leave my place, so I gave him a fit reply.

"Look here Mzwandile you can do whatever you want but never say words you know I will never say. If you don't want to tell me the truth it is fine and if you want to leave It's also fine, but never ever say that I again."

His eyes were wide open, I only use his first name when I am mad at him. I was shivering, my eyes where red. Nick is exactly like Pretty, they never accept when they are wrong. I cried myself to sleep, I don't even know when he left.

"In midnight"

Jack got ready to leave, he had an early flight, so he must go and pack his bags. They both took a quick shower and Jack left. They have promised each other to meet often.

CHAPTER 16

‘ ‘ *The power is when one opens to love, even after heartbreak or disappointment.* ”

Immediately he left Mabusi slept, the poor thing has a long way to go, she will be driving from Durban to Gauteng all by herself.

Around 4:30 am she woke and got ready. She wasn't formal today, she just wore jean with black gold shirt, and sneakers. She checked out the hotel and made her way home. While driving Jack called, he had arrived I guess because there is no network in a plane.

"Hi Jack." She said.

"Mazweli how are you." He said.

Isn't early to call her that but she really liked it though.

"Have you arrived already?" She asked.

"Yes, and I missed you already." He said.

Mabusi kept blushing and her long journey became short. They talked till she arrived and the first place she went to is my place, I am the favorite daughter-in-law after all.

I was watching House of Zwide. I really enjoy it especially the chemistry between Bab Zwide and Rea, those two are not made for each other.

My doorbell rang I went to open, Mabusi was looking so great. I gave her a hug; we sat down and offered her something to drink.

"Look how beautiful you look, how was Durban." I said.

"It was great, really enjoyed my life. Think of going again in December." She said.

"Oh really, please don't leave me behind." I said.

We laughed and I made her something to eat. While eating.

"How are you baby, and how is my child in there?" she asked.

"We're good." I said.

Rubbing my tummy.

"Is Mzwandile at work?" She asked.

"I don't know." I said.

"He is your man; what do you mean you don't know" she said.

"We had an argument last night, don't know when he left, enough about that one tell me about your trip." I said.

She told me everything detail to detail but never said anything about Jack, maybe she thinks I'll judge her or she just waiting for the right time. As our day went by, she had to leave, I walked her out. Got back inside the house and slept on the couch.

As always Pretty did not return yesterday. She was with her other sugar daddy doing deeds. I thought her being positive will mean something but no are does not care at all not even about herself.

Nick on the other hand he couldn't concentrate at work he just kept checking his phone, more like he was expecting my texts or something but no I won't text him first, even if we don't talk for weeks I simply don't care. While in his office his PA came in.

"Hi sir, we have a huge problem." She said.

Her name was Caroline, but everyone was calling her Carol.

"Hi Carol, what's wrong." He said.

"Our client from Cape Town is not happy with the budget we sent yesterday; he says something is fishy." She said.

"Alright thanks Carol, I'll look into it." He said.

Carol handed him a file and left. Something was fishy. The number we not adding up, their profit is less than what they had to get. He started being stressed asked for all the company books. He went through them but could not find anything. He went to Nkosinathi's office to all for help.

"Hey bro please help me out, something is not right here." He said.

He showed files and books to him, Nkosinathi cleared his throat. Got up and closed the door. He was acting strange.

"Nick please sit down; I know what's wrong but please don't tell mom about it." Nkosi said.

"What did you do?" He said.

"Uhm the money I uses to pay lobola I took it from company's profit."

Nick could not believe it; he stood up and placed his hands on his head and Nkosinathi continued.

"I was desperate; I had no money and I wanted to get married. Please bro this can't reach mom, I'll handle this matter don't worry."

Nick was disappointed, he just left without saying a word and Nkosinathi was really scared, what he did was wrong. He should have just asked his mom for money. Now possibility to lose the company is very high. Their finances can't stabilize for long.

Later, after taking a bath Pretty came, she not drunk this time, but she was stinking, more she does not get time to take a bath wherever she is always. She got into her room and took her things. When she came out, I was busy in the kitchen making sandwich for myself.

"Have you found a place to stay?" I asked.

"Yeah." She said.

"Alright good luck." I said.

She left after few minutes Nick entered, I just looked at him and carried on with what I was doing. He went to the fridge, took a beer, and watched TV. He did not say anything nor greeted. When I was about to go upstairs, he asked me to sit next to him and I did.

"Eish, I don't know where to start." he said.

"Start from the beginning." I said.

"I am really sorry, the other night when I went to the kitchen to make you food I bumped to Pretty, she was trying to seduce me, but I put her to her place, and I might have also said something worse." He said.

"And What's that exactly?" I asked.

"I told her that all that energy she is using to seduce me she should use it to take her treatment and said that she is HIV positive, should focus on her health." He said.

"That's explains why she used your things, but why are only telling me now. You'll never stick to your words shame." I said.

"I am sorry baby." He said.

"What else are you hiding from me." I said.

He looked at me and trust me I know that look.

"Can't tell you about this one." He said.

"Alright I will only talk to you if you're ready to talk to me about your other secrets." I said.

I stood up, he held my hand and made me sit down.

"Please don't do this." He said.

"Have I ever kept something from you, have I ever told anyone anything you say so why being secretive?" I asked.

"Ok I will tell you. But please whatever you do don't tell my mom. Uhm Nkosinathi stole some money from the company, he used it to pay lobola." He said.

CHAPTER 17

" T he most important thing in the world is family and love." - John Wooden.

He took a deep breath, me on the other hand I was so shocked.

"No baby your mom needs to know." I said.

"See why I did not want to tell you." He said.

Got up and went to the bathroom. I couldn't believe. The whole mighty Nkosinathi is broke. I felt like letting their mom know but it was not my place to. I went upstairs to look for something I could wear tomorrow I have doctors' appointments. Nick was still bathing; I opened my wardrobe. I took out few dresses did not know exactly what I will wear, while searching Nick came out, I asked for his opinion, and he helped me Choose.

"Are you going somewhere." He asked.

"Yep, I have doctor's appointment tomorrow. You come if you want, gender will also be revealed." I said.

"Eish I'll try but can't promise anything have to fix Nkosinathi's mess, I am also going to the office now." He said.

He was busy getting dressed and I was cleaning my mess on the bed.

"Ok. I was thinking of throwing a party this weekend." I said.

"A party?" He asked.

"Yeah, a gender revel party, at least you can enjoy good news without stress." I said.

"Ok fine with me, only if you don't over work yourself." He said.

He took his jacket, kissed me on a cheek. I went downstairs to watch TV, all channels were boring, so I decided to get my early night. I switched off the TV and all lights then made my way to my bedroom.

Mabusi was taking a nap, her phone rang. It was their client from Cape Town. Mr. Schofield.

"Mrs. Jackson is this how you run a business by cheating us." Mr. Schofield said.

Mabusi was lost, she had no idea what was going on, she sat up straight.

"Sorry Mr. Schofield, I really have no idea what you are talking about." She said.

"I guess those little brats of yours did not tell you what's happening." He said.

"With all due respects you can't call my kids brats. So please tell me what's going on." Are said.

"Ask Nkosinathi he will enlightening you." He said.

He hanged up. Mabusi did not waste time, she wore shoes and drove to their workplace. Nkosinathi was with Nick working very hard. She did not knock.

"Can someone please tell me what the hell is going on." She said.

"What do you mean ma?". Nkosinathi said.

He was really scared, so Nick decided to spill the beans. Mabusi could not believe, she was heartbroken and disappointed. She sat down and Nick made her drink water.

"So, my husband's company will shut down, one mistake, just one." She said.

"No mom it won't." Said Nick.

"Nkosinathi how could you. You could have asked me." She said.

"No mom there must be something that can be done." Nkosinathi said.

"There is nothing that can be done." She said.

"What do you mean mom." Nick said.

She asked both to have a sit.

"When your dad got sick, we had no money for medical bills. So, we took money from the business. Meaning we misused profit for personal reasons." She said.

"Mom why didn't you say so." Nick said.

They were all worried and it was becoming late, so they left and went home. The following day Mabusi woke up very early. She called everyone she thought they could help her but no. Like they say friends are few when the days are dark.

I was in so much pain and Nick is not responding my calls.

"I can't be giving birth now it's only 8 months."

I took my car keys while trying to open the car door my neighbor came.

"Matty what's wrong?" She said.

"I am in pain, please drive me to hospital." I said.

She helped me sit in the car and drove off. We reached the hospital the nurses came running made me sit on a wheelchair and took me to the emergency room. My phone was with my neighbor her name is Siphokazi Khumalo, she's a widow with 5 kids. She called Nick as I requested.

"Hello hey, is this Nick?" She said.

"Yes, and who are you what are you doing with Matty's phone, where is she?" He said.

"She asked me call you, she is in hospital, please come as soon as you can." She said.

Nick hanged up. He left his mom and Nkosinathi, asking questions.

"Nick what's going on." They said.

He got inside his car and drove off. On his way there was a traffic caused by accident, he used another route. Sadly, he made it but not by himself by being taken by an ambulance, he met with an accident.

In the emergency room

I was surrounded by doctors; I gave birth to a beautiful healthy baby boy. It's funny that I was going to know the gender today and I was also planning to have a gender revel party, but God had his plans.

Nick was badly injured; his mother and brother were already informed. Everyone was panicking.

"Congrats Ms. Gumede, you gave birth to a baby boy." The nurse said.

"Really is it a boy?" I said.

I was so excited I've always wanted a boy. Mabusi and Siphokazi met at the reception, they know each other.

"Oh, hi what are you doing here?" Said Mabusi.

"Hi, I am here with Matty, I am waiting for Nick. I guess he sent you." She said.

"Matty! What happened to her, is she OK?" she said.

"Oh yeah, she gave birth to a baby boy." She said.

"Seriously." She said.

"Yes, where is the father I want to congratulate him." She said.

"Nick met with an accident, that explains why he left in a hurry." She said.

Mabusi thanked Siphokazi for being there with Matty when they couldn't and she asked her to take Matty's car with her since they will return with her in Nkosinathi's car, she happily did that.

CHAPTER 18

*T*he new life should bring joy to every family. But now that Nick is not in a good condition, I won't enjoy my parenthood.

As Mabusi entered my room tears quickly filled her eyes. She kissed me on my forehead.

"Thank you, baby, thank you for this gift." She said.

"Don't cry ma, you'll make your grandson cry too." I said

I gave the child to her, she kept kissing him, he was so beautiful and innocent with his tiny hands playing on air. It was a happy moment indeed. I was proud of myself.

"Mabusi was crying non-stop. I could see it was not anything related to the child. Could it be about the company, no let me ask her."

"Ma what's wrong." I asked.

"I don't know where to start Matty." She said.

"Start from the beginning." I said.

My heart started racing, another thing strange immediately after saying that my child cried badly.

"It's Nick, he met with an accident. He's in the emergency room now." She said.

Tears made their way out. This can't be true, my Nick how, when oh God please have mercy. I asked for a wheelchair and went to check on him, but I could go inside the doctors were still busy. 5 minutes after doctor came to us.

"Good morning, Mr Jackson is stable, you can see him if you like." Said the Doctor

That was a relief, I even forgot about my child, he was with Mabusi. I went inside seeing him under machines reminded me of my mom.

Later I was a Mabusi's place she did not want me to be alone besides she wanted to help me.

"Baby how are you feeling now?" She said.

"I'm feeling well now." I said.

"So have you decided what you will name my grandson?" She asked.

"Oh, Nick and I have decided Balekile." I said.

"Why?" she said.

"Because he brought importance in our lifes." I said.

"I hear you, let me go make you something to eat." She said.

Mabusi walked out the room and I left feeding my child. Balekile means important. I was all worried about Nick, hope his health improves soon. While putting my son to bed Mabusi came with tray of food. I ate quickly and went to bed, tomorrow I have a long day I must look for a nanny and go check on Nick, also must attend some class.

As fast as blink of an eye it was morning. Mabusi promised to look after Balekile, I requested for an Uber and went to my place, I changed and took some clothes. Went to Siphokazi to take my car and thanked her for everything. I went to class, then went to hospital to check on Nick.

Today he was better, he even woke up. I went to his ward and he so excited to see me but also surprised to see me flat stomach. I shared the news.

"Balekile's father." I said.

"Wait what?" He said.

"You are now a father of a boy!" I said.

"Baby that's amazing, how is he, does he look like me or you, please tell me?" He said.

The way he was so excited he couldn't hold himself. In few minutes the nurse came to take him to rest room. He took him in a wheelchair, thought it was for that time but nah. After coming back his doctor came.

"Hi Mrs. Jackson, how are you?" she said.

"Hi doc, it's Ms. Gumede not yet Mrs." I said.

"Oh sorry." She said.

We laughed and I asked for updates.

"Oh, I guess Mr. Jackson haven't told you." She said.

"Told me what?" I asked.

"He won't be able to walk, his hips are not in a good condition." She said.

"Will he ever walk?" I asked.

"I can't tell seriously; I'll send the nurse with the discharge forms" she said.

She walked out the ward and left me, yeah, I was happy he was being discharged but it was not easy to understand that he will be on a wheelchair, unable to work normally. After she left Nick got in, I was already packing his bag. The nurse came with the forms, and I signed them. We both left, he just wanted to see his child nothing else, then me had to pretend as if I don't know anything. Wanted him to tell me himself if he will.

We arrived, took out the wheelchair, helped him sit on it and pushed him inside, as we entered his mom got up fast from where she was sitting and hugged him so tight.

"Oh, ma please I just want to see Junior Nick." He said.

"I also want to hug My son." She said.

We laughed; I went upstairs to get the baby. He held him it was a moment to cherish. He was so excited he even shared a tear. Mabusi and I went to the kitchen to prepare something to eat before my interviews start. After some time, the doorbell rang, and I went to open.

"Hi, can I please talk to Matty Gumede." The lady said.

"You are talking to her." I said.

"Oh, my name is Lerato Mokoena, I saw your post on Instagram looking for a nanny." She said.

"OK please come in." I said.

We went in the study.

"So Lerato do you have any experience." I asked.

She handed me her CV along with her qualifications.

"Yes, I have worked in few houses, and I was a primary teacher, meaning am gentle with kids." She said.

"Alright Lerato, uhm I will go through this, and I'll give you a call." I said.

"Alright thank you for your time." She said.

We both got up and I walked her out and sat down with family few minutes doorbell kept ringing and I interviewed everyone. I worked till late the last person left after half past 6. I was so tired; I took a bath fast and prepared dinner. I miss my house already and I asked Siphokazi to look after it.

CHAPTER 19

"There's nothing that makes life happier than knowing your family is happy." - Jayne Mansfield

I kept calling her every hour. After having dinner, I fed Balekile and went upstairs to bath him. After getting dressed Nick read him a bedtime story, I took them videos and pictures. Memories must be created early. I put my baby to sleep, and I ran his dad a bath. I bathed him, helped him dress his Pjs and got him inside sheets.

I also got inside them. Took a book and read it while reading.

"Baby." He said.

"Hmm." I said.

"Well, I have something to tell you." He said.

My mind was like "at least he will tell me without being forced to."

"Uhm I was told that I can't walk anymore but the doctor is not sure if this is permanent or what, but I was thinking of getting a physical therapist but who will work with me at home." He said.

"Baby, I am not trying to be mean or anything, but do you think you will afford it." I said.

He took a deep breath, looked away and covers his face with blanket. I know he is thinking about it, and I will get my respond in the morning. I read till my eyes were burning. I closed the book and slept.

The following day I woke up early, changing Balekile's damper and fed him. Went downstairs to make breakfast for Nick. Mabusi was on her way out, she works hard to save her company. She even approached lawyers but no luck. The company was going to be auctioned Saturday if she does not pay their debts.

I hope I was able to help them, but I can't. I wished her luck and gave her a warm hug. I made breakfast quickly and took some for Nick, I found him playing with Balekile and that warmed my heart.

"Baby please eat fast while I bath Balekile so that I can help you." I said.

I gave him food, bathed Balekile and fed him, after few minutes I helped Nick get ready. I pushed him downstairs. I went through all the CVS I received yesterday while Nick was playing with Balekile. I then decided to hire Lerato, she's the only perfect candidate for this job. Took my phone and called her, she was so excited, and she was going to start tomorrow, sent her my address since we are leaving today. I can't leave here forever Mabusi also need her space.

In the afternoon I went shopping and dropped by my place, I needed to clean before my people come by. Luckily Siphokazi helped me. I cleaned upstairs and she cleaned downstairs so that we can finish up fast.

"I wish we could throw you a welcome home party." She said

"Oh, please not now maybe when I come home with my second born." I said.

We laughed and I made her something to eat fast. We ate and both left. After some time, I reached, Balekile was asleep, Nick was also asleep. I entered the room and started packing our things. While packing Balekile woke up a changed his diaper and put him back to sleep. I carried on with my work. I woke Nick up after and helped him sit in the car, then took Balekile and our things.

I drove off while listening to Take a bow by Rihanna. We arrived quickly, there was no traffic. I helped Nick seat on the wheelchair, took Balekile and some stuff inside the house. I came back pushed Nick inside, put the remaining things in his lap and locked the car.

I gave him remote and went to put our clothes in our wardrobe and fed my baby. I gave birth to a beautiful baby; my son was so smart. He knew the time to sleep and time to eat, he does not even cry unless his diaper is full or when he feels hungry that's all, otherwise he just sleeps without troubling me.

Oh, not to forget I still had a sister. Pretty was planning something huge against Nick and me. This time she was not fighting alone she had someone. Only Nick knows that person, but I'll be the one to get hurt at the end.

Pretty was at the party with some friends. She was then introduced to this girl. Liyanda Johnson. She was a white girl, with blonde hair, tall with blue eyes. They met and immediately they connected. Liyanda was Nick's ex-girlfriend, they dated in high school. She now wants him back.

I was busy looking at the magazine, Nick was taking a nap on a couch, he sleeps a lot lately and Balekile was asleep like always. I decided to take a walk. I was away from home for 5 minutes when I returned, I found a box in my doorstep. I took it and went inside, opened it but I wish I had not, I screamed my tongue out, Nick woke up and Balekile started crying.

"Baby what's wrong?" He asked.

"Look at this!". I said.

I was a dolls head with blood on it more like a doll in the child's play movie. I was so scared I even dropped the box.

"Where does that come from, who sent it?" He asked.

"I don't know, I was taking a walk, when I came back, I found the box at the doorsteps, so I took it inside then this." I said.

We called the police, and they took it, even promised to investigate. I don't think it is saved for my child here, who could do such thing. My mind never rested. I immediately after the police left, I went upstairs to check up on my baby and she was still sleeping peacefully.

"Baby, do you want some sandwich I am about to make some?" I asked.

"No, I am fine. Just get me some water please. Baby who do you think could do this, I am worried about you and my child.

I got him water and ate my sandwich, it was late already, I bath my child and helped Nick to bath too then gave him something to eat while I was feeding Balekile, this little one poop a lot and I hate poop diapers but have no choice.

CHAPTER 20

   " *When you are on chapter 20 of your life, don't let anyone make you feel like you only on chapter 1 because of their inability to read." - Anonymous*

Before sleeping I called Mabusi to check up on her she has been unhappy these days. She was on loudspeaker Nick could hear everything. She told us about the auction, Nick was not happy at all, but he had to accept there is nothing he can do.

   "The company is going to be auctioned because the bank wants its money, so they sell the company to recover the money the being owned."

   Mabusi could not sleep the whole night, she has a day left to repay the bank and her clients, she has already given up. While drinking coffee Jack called.

   "Hey beautiful." He said.

   "Hi." She said.

   "Why are you so down?" He asked.

   "Everything is falling apart." She said.

   She started crying, Jack was so worried but sadly he can't be with her because of distance.

   "What happened, you know you can tell me everything." He said.

   She told him everything, she even told him about the auction tomorrow, Mabusi was so powerless, she was not the same woman I knew. She just gave up. Jack tried encouraging her to fight but it never works.

I woke up early to prepare before Lerato comes. I bathed both my people and gave them something to eat. Nick started acting weird, he shouted at me when I was trying to help him bath.

In few hours Lerato arrived, I introduced her to Nick and showed her around the house. Her job was to take care of Nick Junior and the laundry that's all. Her first day was amazing, there work was not too much I even told her the rules especially letting in strangers. As she clocked out and I was on my way to the mall I gave her a lift. She got off before reaching the mall. I went to mall, brought Balekile diapers and wipes, and some wings for Nick.

After that I went straight home. There was a letter on mailbox with my name. I took it out and opened it inside the house. I was written.

"Watch you back."

I showed it to Nick.

"Baby what's really happening." He said.

I really did not know how to reply to him because I also don't know what's going. Later we did our usual routine, but Nick refused being helped, he said he'll do it himself.

The following day it was Saturday, it was the day of the auction. Businesspeople came and had their seats. Mabusi did not even bother, she was so drunk she was drinking the whole night. The auction started. Nick and I sat at the back; Nkosinathi also didn't come.

"Good morning, ladies and gentlemen, today we've gathered here for the sale of Johnson enterprises the first bet will be R300 000,00," said the auctioneer.

"R300 500,00." Said the lady at back.

"R400 000,00," said the auctioneer.

"R500 000,00," said the front guy.

"R600 800,00," said the auctioneer.

"1 million." The man at the door.

Everyone looked back.

"1.5 million going once, going twice sold." Said the auctioneer.

He got the papers and all necessity. He then called Mabusi.

"Hey where are you, I am around your town." He said.

"Really?" She said.

"Yeah, I can come by your place if you don't mind." He said.

"Yeah, sure let me send you the address." She said.

She took a quick shower, cleaned here and there. As for Nick he said no word since we left the auction. We reached home and Lerato was ready to leave, and our little prince was asleep. So Lerato left and lunch was ready.

Jack finally reached at Mabusi he knocked; the door was opened. He got in and have his woman a kiss on a cheek. He was holding a bottle of champagne and some papers.

"Please get glasses we have to celebrate." He said.

"Celebrate what?" She said.

He passed her the papers with her name.

"What is this?" She asked.

"You won your company back." He said.

"So, you are the man my son told me about, how can I repay you?" She said.

She started being emotional, she shared a tear out of joy. She hugged him and kissed him. Truly saved her legacy, Jack is the best. Mabusi promised to pay him black every cent.

FEW MONTHS LATER

At least the physical therapists are working, Nick is becoming better. He now uses crotches, Mabusi and Jack made things official, and they also became business partners, Nick was happy with their relationship, but Nkosinathi was not. I was taking a nap Nick was looking after Balekile. My phone rang, I answered but no one said anything, I could only hear their breath. This threatening gifts and messages kept going for 2 and half months now.

In two days, it was my graduation day, so I was on my way to the mall to get a dress and shoes. I got off my car as a Diva I am, I visit 3 shops already, but nothing seems to please me so far. I then entered the other shop saw this beautiful dress, it was black with diamonds, I took it, I have shoes that can match the dress so there's no need to get one. I asked the lady working in there if I can fit the dress before I can buy, and she agreed.

I got inside the fitting room, dressed it but it was bit large.

"Sis can I please get another dress make it 30-32 please." I said

And she happy got it for me, she helped me fit it. I bet I was looking so beautiful and sexy. I paid for the dress and went to Boxer to buy my baby some diapers and milk, then got Nick a matching suite and got something for Lerato also. I really like her a lot she's great with Balekile, they get along so well. I knew it when I hired her that she is the best. I was done shopping; I went back home. I reached and got off the car, took out my things and made my way inside.

CHAPTER 21

" *A baby is God's opinion that life should go on. - Carl Sandburg. It's our responsibility as parents to make sure our kids are taken care of."*

I opened the door, and some strange woman was playing with Balekile, and Nick was at work. I thought it was Lerato's friend, I just greeted her and asked Lerato to talk to her about bringing friends at my place without my permission.

"Lerato, I hope you still remember my rules." I said.

"Yes mam." She said.

"So, tell me about your friend there." I said.

"No mam she said she wants to meet with you, so I thought it will be great if she waits for you inside." She said.

"Oh, ok am sorry, you can carry on with your work." I said.

She left; I really don't know this lady here. I went to her and sat down.

"Hi, I'm Matty, I heard you wanted to meet me, you are?" I said.

"Oh, my name is Liyanda." She said.

"Ok Liyanda how can I help you." I said.

"I am here to get what is mine." She said.

"And what is that exactly?" I said.

She stood up and fixed her dress and took her handbag.

"Ask your fiancé who is Liyanda Johnson, you will get your answers." She said.

She kissed Balekile on his forehead and left. I couldn't understand but it's fine. I asked Lerato to leave early today and she did. I made Myself sandwich fast and my baby was watching Peppa Pig he loves them a lot, they are so funny. While eating Nick arrived.

"Hy daddy." I said.

"Hey, my babies how was your day?" He said.

Sat down and carried Balekile.

"It was good, yours?" I said.

"It is great that I am here." He said.

I stood up and went to the kitchen to make him something to eat, while eating I ran him a bath and made my way downstairs.

"Baby what will you like to have for dinner?" I said.

"Pap and milk will do for me." He said.

"Aww really?" I said.

He laughed at me.

"You asked me what I want to eat. Just cook something great baby." He said.

I took his dish, put it in zinc and started cooking. Nick went upstairs to bath; his PJs were on the bed. I just made spaghetti and fish. Hate cooking with all my heart. After sitting down Nick came to watch TV with us, we were watching big mama, but my poor baby does not understand anything. Something started stinking, I knew it was his diaper, I took the clean one and gave it to his dad and put him on his lap and made my way to the kitchen. He had no choice but to change him.

Mabusi was so excited, she decided to tell her kids and workers about the good news tomorrow. Jack had to leave; he had a meeting.

"Baby it was so great being here with you." Said Jack.

"Yeah, it was baby, please visit again." Mabusi said.

"I will my baby. Let me take a bath quickly."

They kissed; Jack went to the bathroom while Mabusi made something to eat. After few minutes Jack was done, they ate, drove Jack to airport. And returned.

It was late already, my baby was asleep but Nick and me we were Still watching TV, but I was tired, and I have a very long day tomorrow, must do my hair and nails the day after tomorrow it's my graduation day.

I went upstairs and Nick followed me, I kept Balekile in his bed and I got in sheets and Nick too. I sat up straight and asked him who is Liyanda Johnson, he looked bit disturbed, and he cleared his throat and looked at me.

"Where does that come from?" He said.

"I found her here earlier playing with Balekile, saying she came to get what's hers. So, who is she." I asked.

"She is my high school ex." He said.

"Oh, so what do you think she wants?" I said.

"I don't know really." He said.

I could see there is something he is not telling me. Slept and faced the other side, his hands started playing down my thighs, pulled me closer I could feel it. It was so hard; he took of my PJs and his too. He rushed mine with his, till action took place. Quickly it was morning, I changed Balekile's diaper and ran his dad a bath then went downstairs to prepare breakfast, while doing so someone hugged me from behind.

"Good morning my love." He said.

"Morning baby, aren't you running late, I've ran you a bath already." I said.

"Come take a bath with me." He said.

"No baby I have to make you something to eat." I said.

"I will grab something on my way." He said.

I tried striking but he was so stubborn, he carried me, undress me, and got into a bath and he joined. We bath quickly, I took out his brown suit and shoes with same color, as for me I took out a blue dress with flowers, with black Nike shoes. I then bathed my baby and made him wear a diaper and took him downstairs.

While eating Lerato arrived, she kissed Balekile and then hugged me. She started doing her work already. After eating I took my phone and handbag not to forget my car keys. On my way out I asked Lerato if she needs anything so that I will get it for her. But she wanted nothing, I went to a hair salon to get my done as usual my hairdresser was late.

"Oh, sweetie I am so sorry, my uber broke on the way." He said.

His name is Sharol, don't know if I should introduce him as an he or she.

"It's ok my baby I just arrived." I said.

"Ok let me change quickly." He said.

He changed and came back. As always, he is the best. Did not want anything fancy just backlines. After getting my hair done it was turn for nails at least I won't have to change anyone's diaper tonight, Lerato will be staying for a night I early morning tomorrow so no one will be looking for Balekile then.

CHAPTER 22

" *The family is the most important thing in the world." - Princezz
Diana*

After getting all ducked up, I went to buy some groceries then
went back home. I haven't heard from my uncle for so long now and that's
not like him. When I reached home my baby was asleep and Lerato was
watching TV, I got in and unpacked then joined Lerato.

Nick was still at work happy that they still having their father's
legacy. Mabusi shared this amazing news with them. But Nkosinathi was
nowhere to be seen even Dr Nandi does not know where her husband is,
he hasn't come home for 2 days.

"THAT'S THE SIGHS OF CHEATING"

I mean why won't he come back home, not answering his wife's
calls and no friend of his knows where he is.

*"Graduating is every child's dream, but it takes dedication and
determination to fulfill this dream."*

The following day was the most important day of my life, I have
waited for this day almost my entire life. It was night already and everyone
was getting ready to sleep, tonight Balekile was going to sleep with Lerato
she requested for him. Before sleeping I tried calling my uncle, but his
phone was unreachable, I then called his wife.

"Hy Matty how are you baby, I heard you ate graduating
tomorrow." She said.

Her name was Nomzwakhe, and she was told about my graduation
by Mzwakhe her son.

"I am good uncle, I am good, yes, it is exciting indeed." I said.

"Congratulations my baby your parents must be happy." She said.

"Thank you. Uhm where is Uncle Mfundo, I tried calling him, but I can't reach his phone." I said.

"Oh, he went to the farms, he was called there but he did not tell me the reason." She said.

"Ok, I just wanted to check up on him. Have a lovely evening." I said.

"OK baby, have blessed day tomorrow." She said.

I hanged up and slept. Without noticing it was morning already, I could not sleep at night, waiting for the sun to rise. While taking morning breath my man came with a tray with food on it.

"Morning Ms. Graduation." He said.

I giggled, sat up straight and gave him a kiss.

"Good morning baby." I said.

"How do you feel about today?" He asked.

"So excited?" I said.

I stood up, went to the bathroom, and brushed my teeth then had my breakfast fast. I did not want to be late, I asked Nick to go fetch my make-up artist and he did while I took a shower. After bathing I called Mabusi to get Lerato a dress on her way, I want her to join us. After taking out my dress the artist arrived. I went downstairs and sat down, and she did her magic, I looked like a doll I was so pretty, while Lerato was getting make-up.

Mabusi was helping me get dressed and handed me a gift box she found on the driveway. It was my picture painting with blood here and there with a letter wishing me the best. I started panicking, they all calmed me down. In few hours we left. We took lot of pictures plus I like keeping my followers updated.

We then got in car, I shared a car with Lerato and Balekile, Nick with his mom and the make-up artist. We reached at the venue and all the graduates were looking great including me of course. My family sat down, and I went to sit down too. In few minutes the ceremony began. People were called on stage, families were happy and proud, some mothers were crying. I also wished mine was here to witness this. As people were called my turn came Mabusi ululated so happily, they all stood up and shout out to me even my friends played the part. I was so proud of myself, at least my child witnessed this.

After all that we went to the restaurant to celebrate, but Lerato could not stay long, she had to go. Her child had a fever, so she just took her order and left.

"Baby I am so proud of you." Nick said.

"Thank you, my love." I said.

"If you hadn't dropped out you will also be a graduate today." Said his mom.

"Yeah, I know but I had to Ma, had no choice." He said.

"Right!" she said.

We had our food while the conversation kept going. Eish at least my wish came true, graduated before getting married. After eating we made our way back home, Mabusi went to her house, Nick left with me. When we reached home it was 6 pm, had no energy to make dinner so I ordered pizza incase if Nick gets hungry. I went upstairs and bath my child and put him to bed, he must be tired after this long day. I took a long bath, wore my pjs and got in sheets and tried sleeping.

While trying to sleep I heard a car driving out of the garage, it was Nick. He was upset about something, maybe it what his mom said but I just hope that is not the case. I tried calling him but no respond, I then sent a text.

"Are you ok? Please call me as soon as you can. Love Matty."

Then I was off to sleep. Balekile cried the whole night, he had a fever. After bathing, I changed my baby and made our way to the hospital. He was not getting any batter. On our way I called Lerato to tell her she should not come today. Also tried calling Nick million time but still not taking my calls. When I reached the hospital, my doctor was busy with the other patient and my baby won't stop crying, I just did not know what to do. After few minutes we were called inside. They did nothing much, just gave him so meds, while dressing him.

"Ms. Gumede, I have been meaning to ask why is Pretty not coming for her treatment, is she ok?" said the doctor.

"What do you mean doctor, I thought she has been coming." I said.

"No, she hasn't she missed 3 appointments already." He said.

"Ok I will talk to her, thank you for letting me know." I said.

I and my baby and left.

CHAPTER 23

" *T*he family is one of the greatest source of joy and comfort." - Pope Francis.

On my way out of the building I met Dr Nandi, we don't see eye to eye lately, she says Mabuli likes me more because I have a child and she can't have children that is why she does not like her.

"Hey Nandi, how are?" I said.

"Hey Matty where you here to meet your Nkosinathi?" she said.

"Wait what?" I said.

"Yes, he arrived about an hour, he over dosed." She said.

Her husband is in hospital, but his mom and brother does not know, how heartless she is. I left with my baby, sent Nick and his mom a text letting them know about Nkosinathi. Mabusi did not waste time she called me, and asked about my text, I simply told her what I know. She made her way there and found her son in ICU.

While in the waiting area she bumped into Nandi.

"Finally, you came witch." Said Mabusi.

She stood up and tried attacking Nandi, but some nurses stopped her.

"Mama!" she said.

"Don't you dare call that, I am not your mother." Mabusi said.

"Fine but is it really necessary for you to cause drama here?" she said.

"Oh, now I am a drama queen, you will know me later." She said.

Mabusi took a sit while waiting for the doctor and Nick. In few minutes I arrived and in some time the doctor came out of the emergency room. His head was facing down.

"Doctor how is he?" she said.

"Sorry Mrs. Jackson, we lost him. The drug he consumed was poisoners." He said.

Nandi joined us and she could tell what is happening by just looking at our faces.

"My deepest condolences Dr Nandi to you and your family." He said.

Everyone cries and as for Nandi she had itt coming her way, Mabusi was already blaming her for Nkosinathi's death. I went with Mabusi to her place, did not want her to be alone in such time. In some time, Nick arrived.

"Hey babe, what happened." He said.

"Hi love, Nkosinathi is no more. I am sorry babe." I said.

"Yeah, how is mom and where is the baby." He said.

"She locked herself in her bedroom, Balekile is with Siphokazi, I asked her to look after him till Lerato arrives. I'll be spending a night with you mom, but I'll check on them later." I said.

He was so broken but did not want to show it. We informed family about the death and the funeral date had to be set. Messages from colleagues and friends kept popping.

Later, I left Nick with his mom and few relative and went to my place to take some stuff for Nick and myself. Lerato was home already she came with her young daughter, Nthabiseng. She's so adorable and beautiful, she was playing with Balekile.

"Lerato thank you for coming at such short notice." I said.

"It's ok, is Ms. Mabusi, ok?" she asked.

"No, she is not really. But she will be." I said.

I went upstairs and took my things, while she was making food for the kids. I left and stopped by to Siphokazi to thank her for looking after Balekile and I drove off.

Things were ugly when I reached there, Nandi was there, the noise could reach the whole neighborhood. I sat inside my car for a while. Nick came out after a while, and he sat with me in a car. I have never seen him crying like that. He broke down.

While trying to calm Nick down we heard something breaking inside, we quickly went in to see what was happening, on the door we found Nandi standing there with her uncle and Mabusi shouting left right and center.

"You are not going to bury my child and I do not want to see you ever again near my house. You are no longer welcome here." Mabusi said.

"But I have the right to bury him, we are married or have you forgot." Nandi said.

"Marriage, you can't be telling me about that. You failed to be his wife. You never gave my son a right to be a father." Mabusi said.

"Oh, is this about me not being able to have kids. We you know what old woman we will meet in court, like it or not I will bury my husband." Nandi said.

She left with her uncle and Mabusi on the other hand was filled with fire. It hasn't been a day since Nkosinathi left us but already there are chaos. I know Mabusi and Nandi never seen eye to eye, but they will have to work this thing out without involving the law, for brother-in-law's sake.

Like they say there is always.

"There can't be flowers without rain, there's always darkness before the dawn, joy comes in the morning."

Maybe tomorrow will be better than today, mother and daughter will let go of their differences. We all went to sleep but I just couldn't, Nick kept turning all night, besides that I miss my baby.

The first thing in the morning, I made breakfast and went to my place, I didn't even eat. I just wanted to hold my child. When I reached there, they were still asleep, but Lerato was doing some chores, o helped her here and there before taking a shower.

After all that my babies were already up, I bathed Balekile and fed him, this one is so smart, he started saying few words even though we don't know he is trying to say but at least we can hear few words, in some words. After all that I took him with me I just hope he will cheer Mabusi, there is nothing she likes in this world than spending time with him and I told Lerato she can go home I will call her when I need her, and she understood.

I dropped them at her place and left after reaching Mabusi's place my baby started crying I think he could sense what's going on, I gave him to Mabusi, they went to her room and came into in few minutes. He was ok, I wonder what she did to my son.

CHAPTER 24

" *Brothers don't necessarily have to say anything to each other - they can sit in a room and be together and just be completely comfortable with each other." - Leonardo DiCaprio.*

Nick came back from the funeral parlor; he was so tired. While telling the adult how he went, I made him something to eat. After that ran him a bath so that he can relax after this long tiring day. After eating he bathe and took a nap. I went downstairs to make tea and do the dishes, Balekile was Still with Mabusi.

While serving tea Liyanda and Pretty walked in.

I mare them tea also, despite having our differences they are our guest, I poked Pretty to talk to her aside.

"Pretty I heard you missed 3 appointments, why do you know how much I pay so that you get this treatment." I said

"How much, I want to pay every penny." She said.

Ok I did not see that one coming.

"This is not about you paying me back, it is about getting better." I said.

"Well thank you for your concern but don't worry about me worry about yourself." She said.

What does that support to mean.

"Fine, so tell Me where you know Liyanda from?" I said.

"I guess you just wanted to know about my health so please mind your own business." She said.

She went inside and left me there. When I was about to get out of the gate Nick called out to me, I looked back, and he came running.

"Where are you going?" He said.

"Taking a walk, want to clear my head." I said.

"Can I join you?" He said.

"Yeah sure." I Said.

We walked together, hand in hand. While we were out Mabusi recovered a letter from court, Nandi did what I have not expected. The court orders Mabusi to come tomorrow, precautions have already been made for the funeral, what will be done if Nandi wins.

Few minutes after the letter Jack called and Mabusi went upstairs to answer it plus it has been a while since Balekile was asleep she had time put him to bed.

"My love are you ok?" He asked.

"Yes, I am, are you?" She said.

"No, I am worried sick about you." He said.

"No don't be." She said.

"Ok I will see you after the funeral because I will be at Dubai for 3 weeks, I won't be able to attend the funeral." He said.

"It is OK baby. I love you." She said.

"I love you too. I will call again later to check up on you." He said.

They hanged up and Nick and I made our way home. There is always drama, Pretty and her friend they were doing the dishes, I wonder what they had planned. And Mabusi seem to be happy seeing Liyanda here, I mean she is her son's ex for heaven's sake. I just looked at them then shook my head and went upstairs to take my baby and my things; I am not needed here anymore plus family was here.

On my way out I bumped into Nick, he was om a phone. He just held my hand while busy talking over the phone. Finally, he hangs up. I went to the car to put Balekile and our bags since they were both heavy.

"Where are you going?" He asked.

"To my place." I said.

"But why?" He asked.

"I am no longer needed here, just want to give people their space and chance to work." I said.

"But I still need you Matty, I just hope this is not about Liyanda." He said.

"Baby you know you can come to my place anytime. Or you can tell me to come to yours anytime my baby." I said.

"My mom also needs you." He said.

With his calm voice and teary eyes. I held his hand.

"Baby your mom is alright now and to be honest she seems happy around Liyanda, so I just have to leave, I don't have anything to do here anymore." I said.

I didn't even wait for his respond just got in my car and left.

"I love him a lot, but I refuse to be made feel as if I am the second best no ways."

It was already late when I reached my place, I took Balekile and our things out of the car and went inside. I putted him on a couch, turned on the TV and he watched the cartoons peacefully while I was making myself something to eat. I ate and went upstairs to take a shower and took a quick nap.

I was so tired I woke up around 8pm totally forgot about my child. I ran downstairs luckily Nick was with him. Just kissed them and went back to sleep. I really don't know what time my people went to sleep but I woke up in midnight because of hunger, I tried standing but I felt so dizzy I woke up Nick and he made went down to made food for me and gave me some water.

"What is wrong baby, you are scaring me." He said.

"I don't know." I said.

"You better see a doctor tomorrow." He said.

"No, I can't go tomorrow, I have to go with Mabusi to court." I said.

"No don't worry babe I will go with her." He said.

I had my food and got in sheets, he hugged, and we slept peacefully. In the morning, he woke up bathed Balekile and made me breakfast. I tried standing again to go to the toilet but still felt weak, I called Nick, came running and helped me and made me get in sheets again.

"No need to go to the doctor I will call him here, you just rest I will call Lerato to look after Balekile." He said.

"Please baby." I said.

I covered my face with the blankets my tummy was hurting so bad.

Nick went to the court with his mom, and it was decided that bath Mabusi and Nandi will bury Nkosinathi together at Mabusi's place. But Nandi was still not happy with the decision taken by the court.

CHAPTER 25

" *A sibling may be the keeper of one's identity, the only person with the keys to one's unfettered, more fundamental self." - Marian Sandmainer.*

Nick kept calling every 30 minutes to check up on me, the doctor was stuck in traffic and pain was bit better, but I felt hot and very weak. I was so sweaty. Nick finally arrived and called the doctor, after 15 minutes he arrived. Did some checkup and gave me meds.

"Congratulations Matty and Nick." He said.

Wait what we looked and each other, confused.

"What do you mean?" Nick asked.

"She is pregnant." He said.

Nick was excited but I was not honestly.

"Wait doc are you sure?" I asked.

"Yes, when last did you see your menstruation?" He asked.

"About 2/3 months." I said.

Oh God I am pregnant; how can I be so careless. Two kids without a job and Balekile is still a child, he's only 10 months old. Where will I even start to mother two kids. I was not happy at all. Nick walked the doctor out and came back. I asked him to bring my baby to me haven't seen him today nor held him. I spend time with him, felt so selfish for having another baby where else he still so young.

In the afternoon I was feeling much better, I went with Nic to his mom's place to check how things were. I asked him to not share this news now and he was so under. We arrived not mention Pretty and her friend comes here every day, they even act as if they are family. I just went to Mabusi had a quick chat with her. I had to get back soon, Lerato must go to her place early today, my baby doesn't have anyone who will look after him and I can't come with him here.

In 1 hour, I reached my place and Lerato left. My baby was asleep, and I took a nap to. In few hours Nick called to check up on me. This one treats me like a child when I am pregnant. I got up and prepared dinner, I just feel like eating real food today. So, I cooked rice and chicken. Later Nick arrived; he had a bath before eating dinner.

While he was having a bath, I was feeding Balekile after that I bath him too then Nick and I had our dinner while my baby was watching Peppa Pig. While eating

"Baby how do you feel now?" He asked.

"Much better." I said.

"Ok." He said.

"Next month it's Christmas don't you think it will be nice if we go on a holiday." I said.

"Yeah, it is a great idea plus we have been through a lot this year." He said.

We ate, then watched TV. Nandi have not come to sit on mattress she is still wanting to bury her husband on her own.

Days went by and it was Saturday already. The service started and still Nandi was nowhere to be seen. Nick and I made our way to the funeral, we wore our black clothes and we dropped Balekile at Lerato's place. When we reached pastor was already preaching. People said their last word to him then we went to the graveyard. Buried him and came back. It was so heartbreaking to see a parent burying their child. Nick on the other side hide all his feelings.

Later everyone left only few family members stayed and Pretty and Friend stayed also. I went to get my child and headed my place, got off the car and took mails from the mailbox, took Balekile and went inside. Putted him down, he's now trying to walk but he walks by furniture. I sat down and opened the mail in my name the rest was for Nick I wonder who keeps sending these threats. It said.

"Congrats on your pregnancy."

No body knows about this pregnancy except the doctor, and he won't share it with anyone. I waited for Nick to get home and show him the letter.

While waiting I changed quickly and started cooking, bathe my child and fed him. He is so naughty these days he slits food and plays with it. I cleaned him up and washed the dishes. Nick finally arrived; he was so tired. He bathed and slept. Didn't want to wake him up I guess I will show him the letter tomorrow.

It has been years since I went to church, I think of going tomorrow. I ate and watched TV with my baby till we fell asleep. We didn't bother to go upstairs we just slept there. I had no strength to carry him, he is so heavy.

Early in the Morning Nandi was on my doorsteps, I woke by hearing a doorbell. I opened and she came inside.

"Sorry to wake you up so early." She said.

"No its ok, where were you? We searched everywhere for you, please sit down." I said.

"How did the funeral go?" she said.

"It went ok." I said.

"Ok I just wanted to know." She said.

She got up and left, she looked messed up. It's like she hasn't slept for days. Few minutes after Nick came downstairs, I left Balekile with him and took a quick shower so that I can make breakfast. After taking a shower I wore my brown full dress, and sleepers then made my way downstairs. I started making breakfast, Nick was not ok it seem as if he was having fever but no it was more. He was battling his emotions inside so that made him sick.

I immediately called the doctor, he arrived after 30 minutes asked him to see therapist or someone he could talk to, gave him injecting and left. I gave him food; he ate and went to sleep. My baby could see that his father is not ok he kept saying.

"Tata, tata, tata."

That's how he was addressing him. I took a walk with him; a lot is happening, and I am worried sick about Nick.

CHAPTER 26

"*Such time should bring family together not break them apart, Mabusi will cut Nandi from the family.*"

We arrived at the park and sat for a while. Mabusi called to check up on us and said she will come later to spend a night with us, and I had no problem with that. We went home and Nick was still asleep, I made lunch and sat down with my child, he was then asleep. Just watched TV alone.

In few hours Mabusi arrived we sat down, and she told me about her day, made her something to eat. While chatting Nick came and sat with us, I told her about Nick's condition. She started being worried, but I was able to calm her down, dished up for Nick and fed my naughty boy. He woke up as soon as he heard his grandmother's voice.

It felt so great to see them accepting the situation. And as for Nick he seems better than earlier now. While talking.

"Ma, we have something to tell you." I said.

I looked at Nick and held his hand, while the other hand was rubbing the tummy.

"Yes?" She said.

"We are expecting." Said Nick.

"Are you serious?" She said.

"Yes." I said.

"I am so happy for you, my babies." She said.

She was truly happy; she even shared a tear. I went to the kitchen to prepare dinner and guess what I was asked to sit down Mabusi will do the cooking. She cooked and we kept the conversation going. After cooking she went to her room to bath. While waiting for her doorbell rang. Nick got up to open.

"Oh God what do you want now?" I said.

"Is it a crime to check up on my pregnant sister." Said Pretty.

"Pregnant how did you know, are you the one who kept sending strange gifts here?" I asked.

"Gift no even if I had money, I won't waste it on you." She said.

I stood up when I saw Liyanda getting in.

"What's going here?" I asked.

"I said I came to check up on you." She said.

"Fine what about her?" I asked.

"She's with me." She said.

"Ok as you can see, I am fine you can leave." I said.

I pushed them both out of my house, I was ok if she came alone, but her bringing Nick's it's disrespecting. I looked at Nick and made my way upstairs, he immediately knew I was angry. I sat on the bed and called my uncle, I needed someone to talk to.

"Hi malome, how are you?" I said.

"I am good Matty how are you?" He said.

"I am ok, I have some news for you. I am pregnant Malome." I said.

"Matty again not that I am judging you, but they haven't paid lobola for you, but you are busy making grandchildren for them." He said.

"I hear you malome, they will pay it soon. Just that they faced some problems uncle. They will call you soon uncle I promise." I said.

"Ok then I will hear from you." He said.

I handed up and laid with my back and faced up. What my uncle just said it is true, Nick must marry me. While thinking he came to the room.

"Baby dinner is ready." He said.

"I'll be there." I said.

He left without saying a word because he knows I'll answer him scrap so he chooses to keep quiet for the sake of peace. I wore my PJs and went downstairs. I sat down, had dinner, and never said a word till we were done. Mabusi asked if I was ok, and I just pretend to be ok.

Even I also don't know what's happening with me, I always feel like crying. Always! I went upstairs sat on a couch and cried my heart out, and Nick made him way to our room. Held my hand and hugged me.

"Everything will be ok my love." He said.

It's funny that he thinks I am affected by his brother's death I mean yes but not to the point that I'll cry so badly. This pregnancy is showing me flames, emotions and moody it's a lot.

He helped me get in sheets, sang me a lullaby like I was a child. He Sat besides me until I fell asleep. Went downstairs to check om Balekile and his mom. The baby was asleep his mom was still watching TV.

"Is Matty ok." She asked.

"Yeah, she is now, she's asleep. I think Nkosinathi's death is affecting her now." he said.

"My poor baby, she will be fine." She said.

"Ok let go put this little champ on his bed." He said.

"Oh no put him on mine, he will be sleeping with me tonight." She said.

Nick did as his mom asked and came downstairs to watch TV with her. It has been a long since they spent time together. I think this time will help them connect even more. They went to bed too late; I did not even hear Nick when getting in sheets.

They say early birth catches fittest worms. Mabusi woke up early and made Nick and myself breakfast, she just wanted me to feel better after last night, they just don't understand it is just hormones nothing more, but I think they will be working my advantage. I brushed my teeth and ate. It has been so long since I had proper breakfast, I always eat brown porridge and cornflakes that's it.

I ate then bathe and bathed my child, I miss him a lot lately even if I go out for some time, I just miss him, and I hope not to neglect him since I don't get to spend too much time with him. I went downstairs and sat with my family for a while, I felt like having pizza, so I ordered some in 15 minutes it arrived.

"Matty you just ate toasted sandwich now pizza." Mabusi said.

"Cravings Ma." I said.

We laughed, Nick came with plates and dished some.

CHAPTER 27

" *Family is one of nature's masterpieces."* - *George Santayana.*
Our little champ kept shouting.

"Pepa, pepa"

His language is not yet clear, but I can understand what he tries to say. My baby wants to watch "Peppa Pig" that's what he wants to say. Well, we changed the channel as per his wish and watched a movie on the laptop, but my boy is so busy he went to the laptop.

We really had good time as family. We even told Mabusi about our Christmas trip, but she asked us to join her in Cape Town and I have never been there, so I see no problem.

Time flew faster than we thought our uncle's met, bride's price was being paid and the wedding date was set. We were getting married before going on a holiday, I have waited long enough. And as for my unborn baby everything was well, he is growing very well. I wish to be him, but Nick wants a girl. He wants to spoil her so bad.

The time for the wedding dress to be fitted arrived, the wedding was in 4 days a lot was happening. My tummy was bit big I had to get another dress. I fitted it, went to the venue to see if everything is still going well. I was so excited that I couldn't even explain it. What I was scared for happened, I neglected my baby. I spent more time busy with the wedding, come late and head straight to bed.

Well one afternoon I to the parlor to get my nails done. I know it is early, but I have lot of work to do plus am doing a of the preparations alone, yeah Mabusi helps here and there. I got home very late; my baby was asleep, and I went straight to bed but couldn't fall asleep. Nick came out of the bathroom; he was taking a shower.

"Oh, hey baby, you look tired." He said.

"Yeah, I am honestly." I said.

"Take a bath, will give you a massage." He said.

I got up and had my long hot bath. Before getting a massage, I kissed my baby on his forehead and sat on the bed. He told me about his day, and I shared my while he was busy rubbing my feet.

"Baby I think we should buy a house of our own, we can't raise our kids in two houses." I said.

"A house with what money?" He asked.

"I was thinking we should sell mine and yours then buy another one." I said.

"Ok I hear you, but don't you think it is too early?" He asked.

"if you don't want to sell your house it's ok but am selling mine and we both going to buy a house together end of story." I said.

Yeah, just like that I was done talking, and he continued with the massage I know he's going to think about it all night long. But honestly doesn't make any sense to have two houses where else we don't use another one, it just visited, and only when Nick and I got into a fight but the then rest of time is spent at my place.

We then went to sleep, around 3 am Balekile cried I woke up, took him, and placed his head my chest, I guess he was having a bad dream. We slept with him in our bed. In the morning, I woke up bathed and went downstairs to prepare breakfast. Balekile woke up I bathe him and fed him. The bed mother I am, I even missed my child's first steps, I did not know he could walk on his own, just saw it when I putted him down and he ran after me crying calling me.

"Mama, mama, mama."

I am a very bad mother. I shared a tear lifted him, kissed him, and hugged him so tight. For a moment it felt good. I made breakfast while he was still in my arms, but he is so heavy. We went upstairs to wake up Nick, he just brushed his teeth and came down to eat with us.

Only two days left for the wedding, and I haven't heard from the Charlie, asked him to design a suit for Nick. I tried calling him many times but no response. Charlie is the guy from my regular restaurant, he also designs. I took my car keys and bag along with my baby and went to his place, and I found his sister.

"Hey is Charlie?" I asked.

"He did not come home last night." She said.

"Do you know where I will find him?" I asked.

"His studio he mentioned something about wedding suit, I am not sure." She said.

"Alright thank you." I said.

I made my way to my car and drive off luckily, I still have his address, I reached his studio, he was asleep and thankfully he was busy with the suit the whole night. I woke him up made him coffee and looked at the suit, it was amazing.

I took the suit and went to fetch my dress. After that my baby and I went to the restaurant to eat some, we haven't spent time together for long. We went to our favorite Hungry Lion and ordered their hot wings for Balekile I ordered something not spicy, while waiting for our order we went to the toy store, he took so many trucks, and I couldn't complain. I paid and went back to the restaurant, shortly Nick joined us. We had our food; my baby was so happy. I just want to spend as much time with him as I can. We finished eating and left, Nick tried taking Balekile with him, but he refused, he wanted to go with me. We got in the car and left. In our way I felt so dizzy Nick was driving after my car. I indicated to stop, he did. He came to my car.

"What's wrong baby." He said.

"I feel bit dizzy." I said.

"Let's do this I will drop you and the baby then come to get your car." He said.

"No baby, I will be fine let's just stop for more 5 minutes." I said.

It must be risky to leave the car here, someone might steal it.

CHAPTER 28

" *A caring husband is one who consistently shows his love and affection for his wife love and* affection over time, through the ups and downs of life."

We waited till I got better, and we left in no time we arrived, I quickly got off the car and vomited. My baby started crying he thought something bad was happening to me. His dad took him inside, came with water for me to drink.

"Are you OK?" Nick asked.

"Yeah." I said.

We went inside, helped me sit on a couch. Nick is protective and there is nothing wrong with me, it's common during pregnancy to vomit I just hope it doesn't happen on the big day. Later, called catering people to check if everything is still fine.

With the blink of the eye, it was the D-Day, the 26 of July. My wedding dresses arrived; the venue was perfectly organized everything was going according to plan. My make-up artist arrived, got my make up done then wore my dress. People were already arriving. I was so beautiful that Mabusi couldn't handle herself, as for my would-be husband he was so handsome in his royal blue suit with brown snakeskin shoes.

The time for the ceremony to begin arrived, Nick was already at the altar. My uncle came and walked me down the alter as always, all eyes were on me. I stood Infront of Nick.

"Greetings to everyone guarded here, today we are here to unit these two souls. Nick I will start with you. Please read out your vows." Said the Pastor.

"I Mzwandile Jackson promise to love and support you, promise to spend the rest of my days loving you madly, I promise to cherish you for the rest of our lives, before our family or friends, richer or poorer, in sickness and in health, for better or worse, I promise to love you and spend the rest of my days with you." He said.

"Matty it's your turn." Said Pastor.

"I Matty Gumede with my whole heart, I take you as my husband, acknowledging and accepting your faults and strength, as you do mine, I promise to be faithful and supportive and to always make our family's love and happiness my priority." I said.

"Nick Jackson, do you take Matty Gumede as your wedded wife?" said Pastor.

"I do." He said.

"Matty Gumede, do you take Nick Jackson aa your weeded husband?" Pastor asked.

"I do." I said.

"I now present you as husband and wife, you may kiss the bride." Said the Pastor.

Everyone ululates we kissed and faced the crowd. The last thing I heard it was people's scream. The ambulance took time to arrive, I had even lost lot of blood. Nick carried me in his arms, took me to his car and took me to the hospital. There was blood everywhere. My poor baby I wonder what he is going through. I arrived at hospital and the emergency room was ready.

Nick was going crazy, Balekile was with his grandmother. My uncle was so worried they were only thinking about the baby. The police were already at the crime scene, Liyanda was the one who shot me. Like she said before she is here to take what's hers, clearly didn't want me and Nick married.

Later the doctor came. Nick was already freaking out.

"How are they Doc?" He said.

"Stable, they are both out of danger. We removed the bullet." said the Doctor.

"Can I see them?" He said.

"No, they should rest, Matty is still unconscious." Said the doctor.

He walked away and left Nick there. He was relieved that nothing bad happened but still worried what happened and why would Liyanda do that. He visited the police station, and his ex was still in police custody. They refused him to meet her. Little did he know that my sister is the master mind of all this, she just didn't want blood in her hands.

"In the interrogation room."

"Liyanda Johnson right, the woman who shot her ex-boyfriend's wife. Why?" said policeman 1.

"I am not saying anything until my lawyer arrives." She said.

"You think you are smart. We have dealt with criminals like you." Said policeman 2.

"And we know you're the one who kept sending Matty threads." Said Policeman 1.

They kept asking questions, but she never responded until her lawyer arrived.

"Gentlemen please excuse my client and I." Said the lawyer.

They both went outside, and Nick was till there.

"Liyanda, I need you to tell me the whole truth. It also states that you were the one sending threatening gifts, Is that true?" Said lawyer.

"I don't know what got into me, do you think there is a chance for me to be released?" She said.

"There are 2% chances only if you had someone working with, we will make it seem as if you were forced to." Said lawyer.

"Oh yeah Matty's sister Pretty she is the one who plotted all this." She said.

"Do you have any messages shared between you two?" He said.

"No, we were staying together." He said.

"That's going to be tough, it is better you confess and say, this Pretty girl forced you." He said.

He left and Liyanda did as he asked, later Pretty was arrested. Nick finally came to see me; I was bit tired and dizzy but seeing him made me feel better. Mabusi couldn't bring Balekile with her since children are not allowed, I'm wards. He sat beside me day and night; I couldn't speak. I was nauseous for few days. But I was in the good hands I know. As for Pretty and her friend they were arrested. Pretty was sentenced for 5 years, Liyanda for 10 years.

After a month and two weeks I went back home, everyone was taking really good care of me. I was visiting the doctor every Wednesday to make sure my child remains healthy. My baby was so sad to always see me on wheelchair. One day he was coming from pre- school he came running to me with painted picture on his hand.

"Mommy, mommy." He said.

He now can speak clearly, and he's so naughty every teacher loves him.

"Hello baby, you're home." I said.

"Mom, I drew you, dad and me." He said.

I looked at it and placed it on the fridge door. I hugged his so tight and send him to his room to change. Then he played with his toys till he fell asleep.

CHAPTER 29

" *P*regnancy is a process that invites you to surrender to the unseen force behind all life." - Judy Ford.

Later Nick arrived, he helped me prepare dinner and invited her mom. Around 8:30 Mabusi arrived, she freshened up and we had our dinner. She was going to spend the night, so she slept with her grandson.

I was sitting on the bed reading a book and Nick was busy taking a shower after some time he finished and wore his PJs. I could tell something was bothering him, I waited for his to get in sheets then I asked him what's wrong.

"Baby what's wrong?" I said.

"I want to apologies for everything you went through baby, it is all my fault. I should have known this will happen." He said.

"No baby it is not your fault, there's nothing you could have done to prevent this. And you're the good husband and a good father to our child, I am lucky to have you." I said.

We hugged and slept in each other's hands. Having the husband who cares not only about your physical wellbeing but also cares about your emotional wellbeing it's a blessing, it shows the amount of love and trust rules around us.

The following day Nick woke up early, made breakfast for me and helped me get ready they treat me like a child. I might use a wheelchair, but I can still use my feet, but Nick and his mom treats me as if I can't walk nor stand, as for my son his grandma took care of his needs and drove him to his pre-school.

In few hours I was all alone at home, I received a call from my doctor asking to see me. I sent Nick a text and he was here in 45 minutes. I sat in the car, and we left. We waited for the Doctor since he was busy with another patient. After some time, we went inside.

"Good morning Mr. and Mrs. Jackson, how are you Mrs.?" He said.

"Morning Doc, I am feeling much better thank you." I said.

Nick was holding my hand so tight impatiently waiting to hear what the doctor has to say.

"So, Doc why have you called us, is everything ok?" He asked.

"Yes, everything is ok, I have been looking at Mattys scans and everything seems perfect, meaning you do not need a wheelchair anymore." He said.

Great news to begin a day indeed, I was so happy. We thanked him and left, Nick never went back to the office, we went to the park, took a walk, and discussed our Christmas trip we once planned. Everything was so perfect, my marriage also perfect, Nick loved and cared for me unconditional.

As for Pretty and Liyanda nothing was going well in their lives, Pretty's health started deteriorating and I couldn't care less, after what they have done to me, they deserved everything bad coming their way.

Months went so fast without realizing, our trip day has arrived. I was busy packing, Nick went shopping with his mom and son, we were leaving later. The nice thing is that Jack booked us in the first class, how rich. I can order everything I want. We then left and reached in few hours, flights are faster than road transports because there's no traffic in the air, how funny. Jack was already there waiting for us with his Bugatti, the guy is very rich, Mabusi is so lucky. We went to his place, WOW! You will never believe he has no wife nor kids; he stays alone with his 6 servants.

We entered the house and could not stop complementing it, he had glass ceiling, the floor was a pure rock how expensive. He showed us our room, I took a long hot bath then a nap, I was so tired. This pregnancy is making me feel old. Later we had lunch then he asked us to change since he's taking us out, except my baby because he's young and won't be allowed in some places.

I wore my long royal blue, with black doek and black hills, pregnant or not I should look sexy and beautiful all the time. We left and went to some casino, he introduced us to few people then we left, I could tell by just looking at Nick that he wanted to play, but I can't let that happen, really can't afford to be married to a gambler no ways. We then went to some tin fish warehouse, we looked around and went to some fish and chips restaurant and ate for free, little did I know all this were his business.

Later we went back to his place, and it was dinner time already, we freshened up and I went to see my baby, he was busy playing in the garden. In an hour we were called to eat, while eating.

"Your place is amazing." I said.

"Thank you." He said.

"You must have spent your whole life building it." Said Nick.

"No, actually my parents left it for me since I am the only child." He said.

We continued eating, had desert, and watched TV. I went to our room to rest; I had a long day. My baby went to his granny crying and asked her to put him to sleep. As for Nick he was busy talking with Jack. Around midnight he came to bed, I was asleep. He got in sheets and started rubbing my tights, I pushed his hands but did not give up. I breathed heavily and he knew I also wanted, and action took place.

In the morning, I was awoken by my uncle's call. He was so heartbroken that I never went to check up on Pretty, he told me how sick she is and I should visit her. I respect my uncle a lot, but I had to reply to him.

"Malume Pretty is old and she knew what she was doing when she tried to kill me and my unborn baby with her friend, and please stop calling her my sister. I am the only child at home, I want nothing to do with that person, even if she dies, I don't care. So, if there is nothing else you wanted to discuss with me goodbye." I said.

I hanged up and sat up straight, Nick was so shocked that I am the one speaking to my uncle that way, but I had no choice. He must understand Pretty has no place in my life anymore.

CHAPTER 30

"*The most important things in life aren't things.*" - *Anthony J.A' Angelo.*

I went to the bathroom, brushed my teeth then bath quickly then joined others for breakfast. Mabusi and Jack were all over each other, I guess last night was great for them.

Nick and I had our own plans for today, we had no worry about the child because he was well taken care of. We are going to use these holidays to spend as much time together as we can because once I give birth, I will have no time to spear for him, plus I must start looking for job, because I'm afraid to ask for my old one to Mabusi.

Well, I wore my light oversized jean and black Nike t-shirt with black and white Nike sneakers. As for Nick he just wore short black pans, same shoes, and t-shirt as mine. We firstly went to the mall, ate ice cream, shopped, went to the museum, went to the park, then lasty went to the cinema. This reminds me of our first date, we got popcorns, went inside then watched the movie. As for Mabusi and Jack they spend the entire day in each other's hands. Later we left and went to Hungry Lion to eat supper since it's late already.

In two days, it was Christmas, the first without Nkosinathi but with Balekile, we had a lot planned for this Christmas, it must be one of the best since were in different location.

After eating my man and I went back, everyone was asleep except Mabusi. I went sat next to her by the pool. We had a chat, she told me how she's feeling about Nkosinathi not being here, I held her hands and told her Nick and I are still here, she should not worry about a thing, and I guess that made her feel better. I went to my room, Nick was busy with his laptop, I took a quick shower then slept.

The next morning, I woke up very early, I had to go shopping with Mabusi for Christmas, Nick had some business with Jack, so today I guess its Girls Day. I bathed, ate breakfast then we left. We first went to buy Christmas Tree and decoration. After that we bought some snacks and drinks then got ourselves something to eat. While eating some old friend of mine came our way, I couldn't identify her but finally I remembered who she is. We shared a meal with her told me she's in cape town for business. It was great talking about high school stuff.

After she left, Mabusi and I also made our way back. My whole body was hurting, Jack called spar ladies, we had our massage session for almost the rest of the day, after that I bathed then slept since I was not feeling well.

Later Nick came to check up on me since I did not join them for dinner. I haven't told any of them I am not feeling well. He came with tray of food, feed me then gave me my meds. He took the tray back to the kitchen then came to sit with me. He kept rubbing my tummy till I fell asleep. Around 2:30 am I woke up, I had a serious pain, woke Nick, and asked for a doctor. He called his mom, helped me change then went to hospital, I thought I was giving birth, but I was not.

They told us that pain was caused by stress, it's too soon for the baby to be born, I still have 4 months to go. We went back and I slept the enter day, I only went downstairs to have Christmas dinner, what the worst Christmas it was for me, and I made other not to enjoy themselves.

Time for us to leave has arrived, it was so sad that I will have nobody to cook for me anymore. We packed and ready to leave, we really had great time.

"I really enjoyed having you around. Thanks for coming guys." Jack said.

"It's a pleasure, we also enjoyed your hospitality." Said Mabusi.

"It's a pity that I won't have anyone to cook for me anymore." I said.

We all laughed, got in the car, and left. In few hours we were in Gauteng already. I was so tired; my baby was asleep I just joined him. Later Nick woke me up.

"No babe you have been sleeping for ages now, are you ok?" he said.

"Yeah, I am fine, just tired." I said.

He ran me a hot bath, while bathing he prepared dinner. I wore my PJs and went downstairs, Balekile was playing with his car toys. I sat down laid my feet on the table then watched TV. Nick then joined us. After some time, dinner was ready, we ate the watched movies till late.

The following day Nick went to the office, as for Balekile I sent him to my uncle's place till new year. Since I was all alone, I decided to go shopping. I bathed, wore brown full dress, same color, and slippers. Went downstairs took my car keys, handbag and left. I reached at the mall, while looking for a parking sport I bumped into NKosazana. To be honest she was totally different. I packed then went to her.

"Hey Nko, how are you?" I said.

"Oh, my Matty, is this really you?" she said.

We hugged and found the spot to chill at. You can't believe she is studying to be a doctor, the very same always drunk Nkosazana, she is even engaged to a man not woman. I told her about Pretty and she was so disappointed.

"I can't believe Pretty could stoop that low. We should hangout sometimes you know." She said.

"Yes absolutely, let me give you my contacts, you'll call when you're free." I said.

We exchanged contacts then left. I went back to my shopping spirit; I shopped few things for Balekile and my unborn baby. The got some for me and my husband. I then went to get some few groceries then passed by Nicks office since I got his lunch.

CHAPTER 31

" *He who cheats for victory, loses twice."* German Proverb.
He was on his office with Caroline his PA, she was sitting on his lap having a moment.

"I missed you, why didn't you call on Christmas?" She said.

"I am sorry, you know I had to spend some time with my family." He said.

"Ok I hear you, so can I please get some now, I missed you." She said.

She said all that unzipping him, when I got in, they were so jumpy like a kid who was found stealing sugar. Caroline came on the other side of the table, took some papers, and left the office.

"Hy Mrs. Jackson." She said.

"Hi Caroline." I said.

I closed the door and looked Nick straight in the eye, he was so scared, I placed the food on the table, then left without saying a word. When I was about to open the door he held my hand, pulled me closer to him. Tried kissing me but I pushed him, I can never kiss lips that was busy kissing another woman.

"Baby, can we please sit down and talk." He sad.

I just pushed him out of my way and made my way out of his office. On my way out I met Mabusi I just passed her without a word, went to Caroline gave her a very tight slap.

"Stay away from other people's husbands." I said.

Everyone was surprised some were not they were suspecting it. I then left, Mabusi ran to Nick's office and called Caroline to ask what was happening. Nick can't keep anything away from his mom, he told her everything. She was so disappointed in them.

"Caroline you better pack all your things, you're fired and you too Nick you broke the rules we had, you know you can't date our employees." She said.

She was done talking, she kept calling me, but I did not respond. When I reached my place, I sent her SMS.

"Tell your son to expect his things, I'll get them sent. And please Ma I am fine just give me some space, don't come. Love Matty."

I packed all Nick's stuff and requested for an uber to send them to his place. While waiting he was on my doorsteps.

"Matty, baby please open the door so that we can talk, you know I love you. I will never hurt you. Please baby open the door." He said.

I never responded until he left, later the driver arrived, sent him the location and he left.

I was so heart broken, never have I thought Nick could do something like this to me. I married him thinking he's different form other men my loving, caring, protective husband, but I guess I was wrong. I cried myself to sleep. The following day I woke up, called my uncle, and checked at my baby. I then got off sheets and took a bath, wore casual clothes, grey full dress, and slippers. I went downstairs to make myself something to eat, while busy someone knocked, I opened, and it was Mabusi.

Every girl deserves mother-in-law like her, I broke down. I hugged her so tight and cried my heart out. She helped m sit on a couch and gave me some water.

"How did you sleep?" she said.

"I don't know really; your son broke my heart." I said.

"I know baby and I am sorry. Is there anything I can do?" she said.

"Yeah, just give me space." I said.

She understood and left; I continued making myself something to eat. While eating Nick called, he has been calling the whole night and I never answered. I booked a spar, wanted to clear my head. After eating I took my car keys, handbag and left. I just found myself at prison visiting Pretty but before she could come, I left. I know I need someone to talk to but Pretty is the last person.

I then made my way to spar for my appointment. I spent half of my day there, in the afternoon I went to the mall, and I met Lerato, we had a quick chat and she left. I also placed an order in Hungry Lion and waited. While waiting Caroline came in with her friends but he she only saw me when I left.

Later I was watching TV, the doorbell rang. I couldn't stand because of tiredness just said the person could come in only if I have known. It was Nick.

"Oh God you got to be kidding me, what do you want?" I said.

I stood up.

"Baby please don't get angry; you will fall sick. Can we please talk?" He asked.

"I said what do you want?" I asked.

"I want to apologize Matty, I know I made a mistake, will you just give me a chance to explain." He said.

"Fine, you only have 10 minutes." I said.

I sat down and he joined me but sat at the other couch.

"Uhm baby I am sorry my love. I know made a mistake. I really don't know what had gotten into me." He said.

"7 minutes left." I said.

"DAMN Matty could please listen to me." He said.

He never shouted at me like this, tears made their way out.

"Mistake, you can't be telling me about mistake. How long have this been going on?" I said.

"Uhm mm." He said.

"Tell me damn it for how long?" I said.

"Few weeks before Balekile was born." He said.

Wow for that long, way before we got married. My married was based on a lie, how can I be such a fool. I stood up and looked straight in his eyes.

"Why Nick why, I loved you with all my heart, but this is the thanks I get. WHY DAMNIT WHY?" I said.

"As men we got needs, you were pregnant, and you denied me intimacy for long, so I guess I got weak." He said

"Get out of my house, Get OUT!" I said.

I went to the kitchen and took out the knife, I did not see that one coming. Slept with other women because I am pregnant wow. I chased him out of my house. Closed the door, sat next to it, and cried a lot. I bet the whole neighborhood heard me.

CHAPTER 32

" *No woman deserves what Nick did to me. But I know I am strong and independent, so I don't need him."*

The following day I woke up very early. Saw so many missed calls from Nick and voice messages but I ignored them and blocked his number, sent my lawyer a text asking for advice the thing is I was thinking of starting my business don't know yet what kind of, but I'll figure it out. In two days, it was New Year, I planned to visit my uncle since I am alone. I will also get a chance to think. I got off sheets bathed and packed, I'll crab something on my way. I first stooped at Mabusi's place, but she was not there I guess she is at work already.

I sent her message since I don't want to meet Nick and his sick kick, so I left town finally. When I arrived, my baby was playing with his cousins when he saw me, he came running. I missed him so much; everyone was so happy to see me. They helped me unload the groceries and offered me something to drink. I took a nap since I was so tired, I had a long journey.

I tried sleeping but I could not plus everyone was busy asking about Nick, had to lie and say he is gone for a business trip. While rolling on the bed I took my phone and watched people's statues. Few friends who knew Nandi posted her; I was so confused but there was "RIP" in every post. Asked what was going on and was told she committed suicide. I could not believe I showed my uncle and the rest of the family, even called Mabusi to ask if she knew but she was surprised as me.

As for Nick he was at his place, playing tv game. Someone knocked at the door, he opened ant it was Caroline, he was pissed to see her but acted as if everything is fine plus, they are equally wrong she can't blame the poor girl, he just opened the door and sat down.

"You shouldn't be here." He said.

"I just wanted to check on you plus you are not answering my calls." She said.

"Caroline, my marriage is on the line here. What we had was nice for as long as it lasted but now it's all over, I want my wife not you so please leave." He said.

"I thought you're different, but you are also like all these men. Now you are done using me you just going to leave me just like that." She said.

"No one used you, you throwed yourself at me." He said.

She just got up and left. He then faced up and regrated all he did to me. Later everyone was outside next to the fire talking and sharing laughs, but my uncle's wife was in the kitchen preparing dinner, I asked if I could help plus it sucks to just sit around doing nothing. After some time, dinner was ready, everyone went to wash their hands. My uncle got 8 kids, so you can imagine how stuffy it is. While having dinner.

"So Matty what are you going to do after giving birth, have you thought about getting a job?" my uncle asked.

"Uhm not really, but I was thinking of starting my own business." I said.

"Alright, what kind of business." He said.

"Not sure yet but you will be the first to know." I said.

"Ok, so will Nick be your partner or you're starting it alone?" he said.

"I'll be alone on this one." I said.

"Please don't forget to give me a job Matty." Said Nokuhle, the 3rd born.

"No, I won't cousin." I said.

We had our meal while chatting. They keep bring Nick in every topic and that annoys me a lot. After eating I did the dishes with Nokuhle and Nobuhle then went to bed. Mabusi video called, talked with her grandson. Though she hated Nandi, but I could tell she was sad about her death, she was her first daughter-in-law after all, and she loved Nkosinathi with all her heart though they failed each other at the end but they really had good thing going on. We all slept.

The following day I took my two cousins with me to get few things for New Year's Eve. I just wore white dress with blue, black, pink flowers and black doek with sleepers as usual. We went to town did some shopping for the little ones, some groceries then went to fish and chips to eat. While waiting for our order Nobuhle went to meet with her baby daddy to get their child school uniform and other things. In no time our food was ready, Nokuhle and I ate with her, we can't wait for someone we don't know when she will be back.

Nobuhle and Nokuhle are twins they're 2 years younger than me and they're the only kids of my uncle I love the most, I could say they are my favorite, we understand each other a lot.

After having our food, we waited for Nobuhle, 30 minutes later she arrived, she packed her food and we left, while driving we were listening to radio.

"To all young women and men who wishes to register their business please visit Young Empowerment.co.za and register your business."

I asked Nokuhle to type that website for me and she did. We arrived and unloaded the things we got from the car, I went straight to my bedroom, took out my laptop the visited the site. I had already made up my mind that I'll open a beauty parlor since I am good with beauty stuff and all plus both my baby cousin twins did beauty at school, so that made things even more easy for me. I started drafting my business plan then emailed it to my lawyer and he helped there and there then I sent it to the "Young Empowerment".

CHAPTER 33

" **P** *ain of a broken heart is temporary and can help us to grow and become more capable of love."*

While busy playing with my laptop my uncle's wife called everyone to have supper, I was not hungry, but I was forced to eat. While eating message pooped on my phone from unknow number.

"Probably I am the last person you want to talk to but please read this message till the end. Matty, I know I messed up big time but please find it in your heart to forgive me, it wasn't my intentions to hurt you but still I did. You and I come from far and I am willing to fight for you, I am nothing without you. You are the love of my life. You paint my sky blue, and you are the only person who strive so hard to pop out smile on my face, you are the mother of my kids, I got to be called dad because of you. You sacrificed a lot for our sake, but I failed you. I love you Matty with all my heart and I'll give you some space but please don't give up on us. Love Nick"

My eyes started being teary, Nokuhle and her mom noticed they sent kids outside to play, my uncle was not at home. They asked me what's wrong, but tears kept coming down my cheeks. I ran to my room and locked myself. After some time, I went to the kitchen to drink some water, and here they were, still waiting for me.

"Sit down Matty and tell me what's wrong." Said my uncle's wife.

I sat down, Nokuhle gave me glass of water. I took a deep breath and told them everything, even asked them not to tell my uncle, he'll kill Nick if he gets a chance to. Well, I went back to my room, scrolled our pictures from our first date to our wedding day, those were really the best days of my life, but I was a fool this whole time. I do love Nick with all my heart, but I just can't forget what he did and move on just like that. While going through my phone I fell asleep.

Pretty was now diagnosed with Aids. As for Liyanda she lost her life while fighting in the bathroom, they stabbed her with sharp toothbrush. Lucky my sister was getting treatment; I just hope she won't let go of this opportunity of getting treatment like she did to me.

Around 5 pm uncle Mfundo arrived from work, he looked so tired and unwell. He took a bath then a nap. I woke up went to the bathroom brushed my teeth then went downstairs to prepare dinner, everyone was on the other house watching TV. I decided to cook uncle Mfundo's favorite, Samp, and stew. While cooking my phone rang, it was private number.

"Hello." I said.

"Hy, may I speak to Matty Jackson please." Said the lady.

"Speaking." I said.

"Ok, I am Joyce from Young Empowerment, we received your application, and I am happy to let you know that your application has been accepted. Please send us all your details so that we can go through them." She said.

"Uhm really! I will send then right away. Thank you." I said.

"Have a great evening." she said.

I hanged up and did not waste anytime I just sent what they asked. A lot is happening in one day, I did not know my prayers will be answered so soon, I thought this will take months but no, not on my case. Thank you, Lord. Continued preparing.

As for Nick he was so drunk he even got into a fight lucky someone on that bar knew Mabusi, he sent her message, telling her to get her son before things get worse. In some time, she arrived the guy was still keeping eye on Nick. He helped her get Nick into the car and they left. While driving.

"Is this how you want to live now, destroy Matty's life now yours. Have you even tried calling her to apologies or talk to your son. I really don't think so." She said.

"Mama not now please." He said.

"Not now my foot, you should be out there looking for a job, have you forgotten you have another baby on the way? You are so relaxed Nick I wonder what's wrong with you." She said.

In no time they had already arrived, they both got out the car and Nick went straight to his room. Mabusi was so disappointed in him. But she got a point even though I don't want to talk to him why don't he call his son. Nick really knows how to get under people's skin. While on my phone my uncle's wife came. When she got in the kitchen everything was already prepared.

"You really helped me; I was so tired of cooking. Nokuhle and Nobuhle never helped me as for Mzwakhe he'll say men are not supposed to touch the pots." She said.

"It's alright, I had nothing to do so yeah." I said.

"Are you ok now?" she said.

"I am, OK?" I said.

"Yeah, about your situation with Nick." She said.

"Oh, that yeah, I am alright." I said.

"Ok sweetie let me get ready for dinner, take care." She said.

She got up tabbed my shoulder and went to her room. I called Baleking but my baby love to play, ever since I got here, he never spends time with me nor talked to me unless he is hungry or want to sleep that's all. I bathed him and changed his clothes later everyone was on the table, just waiting for me, Balekile and uncle Mfundo. I arrived sat down and joined their conversation. They were discussing Uncle Mfundo's surprise party. They wanted to make something special for him this year. He came w had dinner and watched late night movies together. While watching a movie I got an email from my lawyer regarding the Young Empowerment, I had asked for his opinion, so he wanted to check if it is legit or not and the good news is it's legit.

CHAPTER 34

*N*ew year should be celebrated with family and friends especially husband and kids but in my case is worse because it is my first new year as married woman but look where I am.

The following day it was new year, I was awake but lost in my thoughts and still in sheets. While thinking message pooped on my phone, unknown number again.

"Sorry to bother you, just wanted to wish you a very happy new year. I so wish I had not messed up the way I did but I just hope this is our first and last new year apart. I missed you guys. Love Nick."

For how long I will be tormented like this, don't I have to enjoy my pregnancy days with peace more over new year as married woman. Where have I done wrong.

I got off sheets, brushed my teeth, took off PJs and made my way to the kitchen, I was so hungry. My baby was on the streets already, playing. I made my self-something to eat and called Nokuhle but she was at her in-laws, so I asked Nobuhle to come with me to meet with my lawyer regarding the business I don't want to waste time. I know it is holiday, but I just can't wait. We bathed and left. While waiting we shopped some toys for kids.

In an hour he arrived his face was pale maybe he has family problems, who will be pale in new year. We sat down and he took a very deep breath.

"Matty have good and bad news, which one do you prefer first?" he said.

"What's wrong Jerry you are scaring me, the good one first." I said.

I held Nobuhle's hand so tightly, I was even sweating I wonder what the bad news are.

"Uhm I was able to register your business you just need to find a place where it will be and send me the location to send it to them. About the business everything is going according to plan." He said.

"Ok that's great, I am leaving tomorrow I'll get into it as soon as I reach my town." I said.

"Great, the bad one is your sister is no more, she passed on yesterday late. My deepest condolences to you and your family." He said.

"Do you mean Pretty?" said Nobuhle.

"Yes, are you ok Matty?" He asked.

"Yeah, thank you for letting me know." I said.

Though we didn't see eye to eye, but she was still my sister, she did not deserve to die so soon. She had dreams to fulfil and live. God may your will be done, only you know why, and I won't question your decision. We parted ways, I was silent the whole trip. I can't even cry thinking of how she turned my life up and down, firstly slept with my husband, pushed me, and killed my child, stole from my house, made my life so hard by sending threatening gifts and messages, invited Nick's ex in our life then they tried to kill me. Theres nothing good to remember about her.

We reached and I went straight to my room, locked the door, and threw myself on the bed. I felt so sad that I started packing my bags. I wanted to visit the prison she was at and ask why I was not told about my sister's death. Nobuhle told everyone about Pretty's death. I opened the door called Balekile to bathe him, but Nomzwakhe refused me taking him, well that's minus one problem. I took my bags to the car, while in the car.

"Baby I will and get you soon ok, and please don't bother your cousins and grandma too much." I said.

"Ok mama." Balekile said.

"Mama loves you ok, behave." I said.

He left, Nobuhle and her mom hugged and wished me a safe trip. I then drove off. While driving I got a call from my doctor. He wishes to meet me and Nick as soon as possible, its regarding the baby. If I had high blood surely, I would have collapsed. So many bad things in one day. I reached my place, freshen up. Unblocked Nick and called him. I called 3 times but no respond, asked his mom where he is but she also didn't know so I decided to go to his place.

While packing my car I saw police van and heard some noises, more like people were fighting. I got off the car quickly and went inside. Men never change. It was him, Caroline, and the police, I got in slowly.

"What's happening here." I said.

"Mam this is privet matter please leave from here." Said Policeman 1

"You are in my husband's house, and you ask me to leave." I said.

"Sorry Mam I didn't know." She said.

"Can someone please tell me what the hell is going on." I said.

"Someone pressed charges against your husband." Policeman 2.

"What are the charges?" I said.

"Rape." Policeman 1

"What and she is that person pressing charges." I said.

"Yes mam." Policeman 2.

Her seeing did not make her happy because she knew she is going to fail on this one.

"Oh really, when was she raped, did she tell you my husband and I live separately because they were having affair, did she tell you that." I said.

"No, she did not mention the affair she said she was raped 1 month I go." Policeman 2

"Oh really, please stop wasting your time and the government resource for nonsense." I said.

"Ms. Caroline, were you raped or not." Policeman 1.

"It is more like rape because he slept with me and then left me just like that." She said.

"No, it is not, Mr. and MRS Jacson were sorry for disturbing your peace. Enjoy your new year."

They then left; she was facing down all the time because of shame. Told Nick why I was at his place, he tried thanking me, but I did not want to hear a thing I have gone through too much already.

CHAPTER 35

*M*y husband and I have totally become strangers, were barely talked nor looked at each other. It is funny to think how in love we were not so long ago. But it is what it is.

We reached at hospital, got in and sat down. Luckly, he had no patients. We waited for him while he was going to get my scans. He sat down and took a deep breath.

"I wonder what is wrong with everyone taking deep breaths today for God's sake I am 8 months pregnant."

He took out the scans and showed them to us, I could not understand a thing, so I asked him.

"Doc is everything ok?" I said.

"I wish I could say so, do you see that thing like a rope." He said.

"Yes." We said.

"That's your umbilical cord, it goes around your child's neck, and he might not survive." He said.

I am sure I did not hear him clearly, so I sat up straight and asked him to repeat that again. I can't lose another child. My eyes started being teary.

"So, what can be done to save our child." Said Nick.

"We need to do C-section, the child might be tiny, but he will leave in an incubator until he is fit to go home." He said.

"Is that even possible, when will I have to do the operation doc?" I said.

"Anytime but don't take too long, at least by the end of this month it should have been done, there's nothing to worry about because both you and the baby will make it alive." He said.

"Alright thank you." We said.

We got up and left the office, I was so down I couldn't believe a thing. I got in my car and drove off; I left Nick there I wanted someone to blame. I passed by the prison and had a word with warden.

"Hey, I am Matty Jackson can I please meet Warden Moloi." I said.

"Hey Ms. Jackson." Said the lady.

"Mrs.!" I said.

"Ok Mrs. Jacson, Mr. Moloi is not available, he's in a meeting." Said the lady.

"When will he be available." I said.

"I don't know." She said.

"Alright, here's my card please give it to him and ask him to call me when he gets a chance." I said.

"Ok I will." She said.

I then got in the car and left; I drove around the city just to clear the mind. While driving Uncle Mfundo called I guess they had told him about Pretty. His voice sounded bit down, but he had accepted since he saw how Pretty was suffering. I told him I just visited the prison to ask the warden why he did not tell us about Pretty and he was not pleased at all. I finally arrived at my place, got inside, and tossed myself on the couch.

One thing I like about myself is that I am strong, I handle things without breaking. I consider myself to be a phenomenal woman.

I don't know when I feel asleep, but I woke up by hearing my doorbell ringing, I got up to open and it was my uncle, his wife and Nobuhle. I welcomed them happily like they welcomed me and my kid to their house, I offered them something to drink and Nobuhle took their bags to their rooms. They left the kids with Nokuhle so there is nothing to worry about. We sat down and discussed Pretty's funeral, while talking Mabusi walked in. she was so happy to finally meet my uncle's wife and kid. They had their conversation while Nobuhle and I prepared dinner and uncle Mfundo went to his room to take a nap. Mabusi called me and told me how well Nandi was buried, and her family welcomed her with love, there were no fights at all, I was so glad to hear that finally. I told her about Pretty though she never understood her she passed her condolences and was bit heartbroken. In no time dinner was ready, my uncle joined us and Mabusi stayed for dinner. While eating.

"OH, before I forget, I am getting married," said Mabusi.

"Wow Ma really, I am so happy for you." I said.

We all congratulated her, truly speaking I am happy for her. Jack has been a real guy to her, they treated each other with love, care, and affection. Well, it was late so I asked her to stay, Nobuhle will sleep with me since all rooms will be occupied.

The following day I woke up early, called my doctor, told him to make me an appointment for the operation and he was pleased to hear that, also informed Nick maybe he wants to be there who knows! the operation was in two days. I got off sheets, brushed my teeth and went downstairs. I started cleaning my house and prepared breakfast for everyone. While preparing breakfast Mamzwakhe came out her room and helped me there and there. As for my slay queen mother-in-law she was deep in dreams as always. I made her and uncle Mfundo tea and sent them to their rooms.

It was decided that Pretty's funeral will be held at my uncle's place so that she can be buried near her mom. I just hope she will rest in peace she troubled us a lot when she was still alive.

After all that I went to my room to wake Nobuhle and take a long hot shower. I got inside the shower and relaxed my body while thinking of this whole thing. After some time, they called me downstairs, I got out of the shower, put on some lotion then wore while dress with grey t-shirt and slippers as always. Went downstairs everyone was having their breakfast my uncle excluded. He went to the funeral parlor to prepare for Pretty's funeral. He has a lot going on already, I wonder how he will react upon hearing about my operation in two days, surely, he is going to have heart attack, he is too old this will be too much for him and I can't hide it from him because he will see me with a flat stomach on Pretty's funeral and he will start asking questions.

CHAPTER 36

" *Your pain is breaking of the shell that encloses your understanding." - Khalil Gibran.*

Around 3 pm my uncle arrived, I was busy doing Nobuhle's hair, his wife was out with Mabusi. He was so down he sat down, Nobuhle got up to make him something to eat. Everything was now prepared for the funeral, Pretty's body will be transferred to KZN tomorrow, they will also leave. While eating.

"Uncle there is something I need to tell you." I said

"If it's about Nick Nomzwakhe has already told me." He said.

Hoo his wife can't keep secrets shame, this whole time I thought he knows nothing, but I was fooling myself.

"No, it's not about him, but about the baby." I said.

He stopped eating and looked at me. Nobuhle also sat still.

"The Doctor said my baby might die; he has an umbilical cord around his neck, so I need to make an operation to take the baby out. He will be staying in incubator until he is fit to come home." I said.

"Matty when is the operation?" he said.

"In two days." I said.

"But Mzala the funeral will be in 3 days will you be able to attend?" said Nobuhle.

"Yes, I will." I said.

They were so worried about me, Uncle Mfundo reacted the way I did not expect, he always shouts though it is not our fault something happened, but he shouts. I got up made so juice and made my way to my room. Just as I sat on my bed, I received a call from the prison.

"Matty Jackson hello." I said.

"Hello, you are talking to Mr. Moloi, my receptionist told me you were here to meet me." He said.

"Oh yeah. I wanted to know why when Pretty Gumede died no one from her family was informed." I said.

"We tried calling you mam, but your phone was unreachable." He said.

"No, you must be lying because I never switched my phone off or something that will make it unreachable." I said.

"I hear you Miss Matty, we are sorry for that." He said.

I hanged up. Laid in my back and faced up, while lost in my thoughts Nick entered my room. He came with his mom, and they were not staying. I sat straight, he came and sat next to me.

"Hy, how are you feeling?" he said.

"I feel pregnant and tired, you?" I said.

He took a deep breath handed me the letter in his hand and left. I wonder what's written there, or is it divorce papers. I kept it in my drawer unread. To be honest my mind was giving me the worst, so I decided not to read it. Later I went downstairs dinner was ready, but my uncle and his wife had to go since they will be the one to welcome Pretty's corps, so they were not able to join us. Nobuhle stayed behind to help me after the operation since I am all alone. We had our dinner and went to sleep.

In the blink of an eye, it was the operation day. Uncle Mfundo called me early to pray for me and wish me luck. Nick also came bit early to go with us since I can't drive. I got ready and wore casual. We left and I was so nervous. Nobuhle was holding my hand so tight, thankfully my child was not here otherwise I was going to be so worried about him. We reached and the operation theater was ready.

I went to the toilets to change, and everything was ready. The operation went on for almost 3 hours and Nick was already losing his mind, he kept going up and down, every nurse or doctor that comes out he runs to it to ask for the updates. While waiting my doctor approached them with smile.

"Congrats Mr. Jackson you are blessed with a baby boy, everything went very well both mother and a child are ok." He said.

"Oh, thank God, can we see them?" he said.

"Yes, but please don't wake them, they need to rest." He said.

The doctor left them, Nobuhle called her father and told him the great news, Nick also informed Mabusi then they came to see me. I was still unconscious. Nick held my hand and kissed it.

"Thank you, baby, for this gift. I don't deserve you really." He said

After some time, the nurse came and asked them to fill some forms at the reception and Nick went to do that. In some time, I opened my eyes Nobuhle was next to me, I smiled at her and looked the other side to see my baby, he was so tiny and handsome just like his father, light skin and he had Mabuse's blue eyes. I sat up straight and the nurse gave him to me. Every time holding a newborn feels so great, I knew we are going to get along so well. I was only allowed to hold him for 5 minutes.

The other part of me was so excited about the baby the other was so worried about the funeral tomorrow and to leave my baby all alone here. Finally, Nick got in we must discuss the child's name. since he is the one whole named the first born, I thought it will be fair for me to name this one, so I named him Ifalethu, it is a beautiful name and his dad just agreed with me. Later around 4 pm I was discharged, I asked my doctor to take a very good care of my baby. Jack even hired a nanny to look after the baby while we are gone. We left immediately when the nanny arrived, we have a very long way to go, and we arrived around 9 pm. I kept calling the nanny every hour to ask about the baby, I guess that's how all mothers react.

I was sitting on the car and my uncle came to ask why I don't get inside. I had no Courage to; and I broke down. Nick held me so tight and told me all will be well. I was feeling so sad that she died while I was still mad at her. He went inside with me,

CHAPTER 37

*L*ike they say death is the bride of all homes.
It was the next day. Everyone woke up early and got ready to see the dead, but I refused to. It was such a heartbreaking moment to experience. We all went in the tent for the service to begin, the box also came out and everyone started singing. Friends, family, and neighbors spoke.

"It feels as if it was yesterday when we went to school together, did our homework together and got admitted at varsity. Though you and I never saw eye to eye you were still my sister and I still loved you. I hope you forgive me if I wronged you unknowingly and please greet our parents and rest in peace. We are still and will always love you." I said.

We then took her to her final rest place. It was so painful to see my uncle cry like that, but I had to be strong. As for the operation pain I kept taking pain killers now and then which is not healthy.

We went back, everyone ate. I couldn't wait any longer. Nobuhle took her other clothes and my child's too we were leaving with him this time. I forgot to tell Balekile was so happy to see his dad and he never played since then but when I got here for Christmas, he was too busy for me. We drove off and we went to the hospital first to check on the baby. Children were not allowed in wards, so Nobuhle stayed with Balekile in the car while Nick and I went to see ifalethu. My baby was asleep with all pipes and machines around him. I just hope he gets out very soon. We held him for some time then left. While driving.

"Mama sis Nobuhle says I have a baby brother." He said.

I looked at nick and giggled then looked at the back.

"Yes, and his name is Ifalethu." I said.

"So, I am no longer your baby." He said.

"You are still and will always be my baby." I said.

My baby feels threatened by his baby brother's arrival, he feels as if we will love him less and that's not the truth. It hurts seeing him feel that way. We then arrived at my place, the only thing I wanted to do is to get a hot shower, take a nap then visit my baby. I got off the car, carried Balekile if it will make him feel batter then got inside. I sat on a couch, stretched my legs, and took a deep breath with my head facing up. Nobuhle and Nick they were busy taking our things out of the car and joined us. Nobuhle went upstairs with Balekile and Nick was watching TV. It was a very tense moment.

"Uhm, I wanted to thank you for driving us to the funeral." I said.

"It's ok, I also wanted to go you know and support you." He said.

I looked at him and signed.

"Did you read the letter I gave you." He said.

"No, I haven't had plenty of things to do so I never got time to, what's written there." I said.

"Ok please do you will find out." He said.

He then got up and left I was so sure this time that it is divorce papers. I got up, ran to my room and to the letter out of the drawer and rend it. What a relief, just his WILL, is he dying soon or what. And I don't think it was needed for me to have a copy of his will, but it is what it is. I got undressed and took a quick shower, wore black tracksuits with black and while Nike sneakers, took my car keys and went to Nobuhle's room, they were asleep with Balekile, just wrote a note and left if on a freezer. I drove off and went to the hospital to see Ifalam, he was still ok with his little fingers playing around my face.

Around 8:24 pm I left the hospital and went straight home. Mabusi was also at my place to ask how the funeral went, she could not come since she had to leave the city because of the business meetings. Well, we told her every detail later after having dinner she left. Nobuhle was watching TV, and I was packing some stuff for Balekile, Nick decided to spend some time with him before schools opens. While packing he arrived sat a bit and left with his son. I also joined Nobuhle, but I was busy with my phone looking for a place for my business, while looking I just remembered Mabusi's building, they do not use the first floor and I don't think she will deny my offer. I texted her immediately and she responded. We don't need to be offended by somethings but her turning me down was something else.

Months went by and my cute ifalethu was home too, he was growing so well. Him and his old brother get along very well, my business was also doing well, Nobuhle was my business partner. My relationship with Nick was good, we had fix things between us and not to mention I am always all over the newspapers and internet because I am now the face of Young Empowerment. They loved my work a lot. A lot has happened these past few months.

It was Friday and the salon was busier than the other days had to help there and there but finally my time to leave arrived, had to get my kids from school so I left Nobuhle in charge.

They say do not combine family and business, but I say just find the one with good intentions, Nobuhle was so dedicated and determined in what she is doing. I never regretted making her my manager because I knew what I was getting myself into.

I finally reached the day care center, went inside, and took my kids and left. It was Balekile's birthdays in few days, so his dad and I had decided to throw a party for him. My baby was a very responsible brother, his teachers say every hour he goes to check on his little brother. In no time we arrived, Nick was not at home, he was still Job hunting he hasn't worked since his mom fired him.

CHAPTER 38

*T*he bond between my kids is the bond I have always wished to share with Pretty but we failed to.

I took out the meat from the freezer to be cooked for dinner, bathed Ifalethu, Balekile then fed him while I was busy at the kitchen someone knocked at the door.

The brother of the house went to open it and it was my lawyer what a surprise. I offered him something to drink, Balekile took ifalethu to play in his room while I had a chat with my lawyer.

"Hy Matty." He said.

"Hi, what a pleasant surprise." I said.

"No man I was in the neighborhood so thought I should come and give you the feedback regarding your request." He said.

"Ok!" I said.

The thing is I decided to buy a house and sell mine because we need more space though Nick did not contribute but I had no problem with that.

"Uhm, you requested for a house with 5 bedroom, 2 baths rooms, 1 or 2 study rooms, kitchen, dining room and sitting room with 2 doors garage." He said.

"Yes." I said.

"I got the better deal, same bedrooms, 1 bathroom but the master bedroom has its bathroom, 1 study, playing room, kitchen, dining room, sitting room and same garage with only R100 000." He said.

"What R100 000 where will we get so much money; my husband is still unemployed plus we haven't found buyers so how will we manage all that." I said.

"I thought you are smart Matty. You are the face of Young Empowerment, right?" he said.

"Yes." I said.

"There is nothing to worry about they will pay for your house." He said.

"Really?" I said.

"Yes, I will email you the contact and show it to your boss then I will take it from there." He said.

Only if I knew early, I would have been leaving in my dream house, my parents must be proud wherever they are. He took his bag and left, and I carried on with my work. Later Nick arrived, kissed me on the cheek then went upstairs to check up on his champs. After cooking I went to my bedroom took out Nicks Pjs and placed them on the bed while he was busy taking a bath. Went to Balekile's room, they were busy playing, and I went to set up the table.

After some time, everyone came downstairs to eat dinner, while eating I told Nick the great news, he was so excited, we even decided to do the house view tomorrow plus it has been so long since I spent some quality time with my man. We ate and all went to bed, Nick read bedtime story to the kids while I was taking a shower. He then came to our room, he got in sheets, and I joined him after getting dressed, massaged him. He was so tense, and I didn't even want to bother him about his problems.

I kissed him in his neck, went down on my knees then went back to his lips. I made him forget about the world just made him think about me and him. Things started getting hot, his hands played on my tights till action took place.

The following day I woke up early because I had to take care of few things at the salon before the house view. I made breakfast, cleaned here and there since there were toys everywhere. I woke up Balekile, bathed him then his little brother then woke my man with breakfast in bed, how romantic. I went downstairs fed my baby and packed their bags. Took a very quick shower, asked Nick to drop kids at school (Crèche). Took my car keys then hit the road. While driving I was listening to Eminem, kinder like him lately. Finally reached, Nobuhle was running late but luckily, I had a spare key, opened then did my job. Looked at the books and some touch up here and there. Around 9:39 she finally arrived. She now has a boyfriend whom she lives with, and they are treating each other so well. I asked her to take care of some stuff for me today since I won't be available the whole day. It is nice to be your own boss. I then left.

I was driving down a quiet, tree-lined street. The houses are neat, lawns were well manicured and had flowers. They had sidewalks and streetlamps, and the air is filled with the sound of birdsong. The neighbourhood has a welcoming feeling, and it was peaceful and friendly. It seems like the perfect place to call home.

When I arrived, Nick was already there, I sat in the car for a moment as I pulled up in front of our new house. By just looking at the house I kept smiling, but Nick seemed bit nervous. I finally got off the car and approached him.

"Baby just look at our new home." I said.

My voice was full of excitement.

"It's perfect, isn't it?" I said.

Nick did not answer right away, I could see he is not himself. I reached over and took his hand in mine.

"What's wrong dear. Don't you like it?" I asked.

" No, it's not the house, it's just a big change, you know. Moving to a new place, starting over, it is bit overwhelming." he said.

I squeezed his hand.

"It is ok to feel nervous and bit worried, but this is going to be a wonderful new chapter for us. Just think of all the possibilities." I said.

He smiled and nodded.

"You are right, I am just overthinking." He said.

I smiled back at him.

"Come on, let's go inside." I said.

We stepped through the front door of our new house. The entry room was bright, with a staircase leading to the second floor. To our right was the living room, with large windows looking out the front yard. Straight was a dining room, with space for a table that could seat eight people. On our right was the kitchen, with gleaming countertops and stainless-steel appliances. Nick and I looked at each other, our eyes were wide with wonder. I could already imagine the life we would build in this house. I signed where needed then the house was mine.

CHAPTER 39

" *T*he ache for home lives in all of us, the safe place where we can go as we are and not questioned." - Maya Angelou.

One month later, the house was starting to feel like home, we had unpacked all the boxes, put up pictures on the walls, and arranged the furniture to their liking. I had even planted some flowers in the front yard. As we sat down for dinner Nick looked at me.

"I am so glad we moved here. It feels like a fresh start for us." He said.

I smiled and nodded in agreement. The house was so child friendly, and my kids were loving it. Not to forget we could not celebrate my son's birthday there because we had to move but managed to celebrate it earlier today. after this long tiring day, I was in the kitchen, trying to clear up after the party. The birthday cake was in the fridge, the presents are scattered around the living room, and there are toys and wrapping paper all over the floor. I was exhausted, but I know I must clean.

Suddenly, I heard a strange noise coming from upstairs. It sounds like something is moving around in the empty room. I decided to ignore the noise and figured it is probably just the wind or an animal. I took a deep breath and starts cleaning up the mess from the party. As I was picking up the toys and putting them in a basket, I heard the noise again. This time, it sounded like footsteps. My heart started racing. My hands were shaking as i put down the basket of toys. I tries to tell myself that it is not nothing to worry about, but I can't shake the feeling that something is wrong. I walked over to the stairs and slowly starts to climb them. The footsteps were getting louder. I reached the top of the stairs and stares at the room's door.

Went to my room slowly and silently asked Nick to come with me and while trying to deny he also heard the sound; he then took his golf stick and approached the room. I reached out to turn the doorknob. With a deep breath, I turned it and pushed the door open. The room was dark and dusty, and the only light came from the moon shining through the window. Suddenly, the footsteps start again, this time louder and faster. Guess what it was. A pack of rats, we breathed in relief. Nick used the golf stick to shoo the rats out of the room. It was now quite again, and we closed the door. went back to our bedroom and throw myself on the bed.

"Well, that was scary, but at least it was just rats." He said.

I laughed and nods in agreement.

"I hope they don't return." I said.

Since I was tired and had no energy to continue cleaning just decided to sleep. We both got a good night sleep, knowing that the other room is free of rats and other mysterious creatures. And I should get enough sleep still have lot of work to do.

The following day my poor husband woke up very early because he knew I will be tired after yesterday's work. He made me a cup of coffee, run me a bath and bathed both kids. After my bath breakfast was already served, I wore my long blue, pink dress with white t-shirt and black sneakers then combed my afro hair then had my food. After eating I kissed my 3 babies and left, I was late already. As soon as I left Nick got the kids ready and took them to school.

I have back-to-back meetings and tasks ahead of me. As the day goes by, i managed to get everything done despite the hectic start I had. At the end of the day, I was exhausted but satisfied, knowing that I accomplished everything set out to be done. I still had a photo shooting to attend after work. One hour later I arrived at the studio feeling bit drained from the long day, but the photographer was able to put me at ease and made me feel comfortable in front of the camera. The photoshoot went well, and I left feeling energized and excited about the pictures.

As I tossed myself on the Couch my loving husband took feet and placed it on top of him and massaged them.

"How was your day honey?" He asked.

"Tiring but worth it, yours?" I asked.

"Just normal. So how did the photoshoot go?" He asked.

"Eish it was great, i even learnt few things like how important it is to feel comfortable and confident in front of the camera. The photographer really helped me to relax and just be myself. I also learned that it is okay to make mistakes but to be honest today's pictures were the best." I said.

"That's amazing." He said.

"And your day with the boys?" I asked.

"Uhm, my day with the boys was so much fun! We went to the park and played on the swings, the slide. They were so full of energy and laughter, and it was so much fun watching them play. We even had a picnic lunch and told them some stories. Let me say it was the perfect day." He said.

As even draws closer, I had to prepare dinner, but Nick could not let go of me. I guess He just miss spending time with me.

"I am so grateful I have you." He said.

"I love our life together." I said.

I then got up made something fast, we had dinner and went to bed. Only God knows when we fall asleep in each other's arms, with smiles on our faces. While sleeping Balekile shouted

"Mommy, Daddy! The baby needs you!" He said.

I got out of the bed with difficulty and headed to Ifalethu's room. When I opened the door, he was lying in the crib, looking sad and waving a soiled diaper around. while changing the diaper, he started talking and laughing, making it hard for me to focus. Nick then walked in with the bottle and sees the scene of me struggling to make Ifalethu wear clothes. He started laughing, the then fed him, after some time he finally fell asleep, went back to our room and had a chat for some time then got in sheets and fell asleep in each other's arms, peacefully and happy.

CHAPTER 40

" *Uncles are there to help the child get into mischief that they can't get into with their parents." - Unknown.*

The following day I was sleeping peacefully then message popped in my phone. I was still bit sleepy, took it and read the message. I sat up straight to process the information. Nick woke up and saw me sitting up straight, staring at my phone. He can tell something was wrong.

"What's going on?" He asked.

His voice was deep with sleep. I looked at him, my eyes were full of tears.

"I…I got a message. My uncle…he. He is gone." I said.

With my shaking voice he reached out his hand and took mine, pulling me close.

"I am so sorry honey, tell me what happened." He said.

I took a deep breath and began to tell him about the message.

"It was from his wife, she said that my uncle had a heart attack last night, and he could not make it. He is gone." I said.

He held me closer, letting me cry into his shoulder. After a few minutes, I calmed myself down and continued.

"I can't believe it, uncle Mfundo was always so full of life. He was always the life of the party, and he loved making people laugh. He was such a big part of our family." I said.

Nick listened as I talked about my uncle and the memories, I had of him. Telling stories of family gatherings and holidays and talked about how much he loved his nieces and nephews.

"He was always so generous. He would do anything for anyone. He was such a good person." I said.

As I was talking Nick could see how much my uncle meant to me. He knows that I was going to miss him terribly.

"Are you going to be, okay?" He asked.

I took a deep breath and wiped my face.

"I am going to miss him so much, but I know he would not want me to be sad. He would want me to remember all the good times we had together, and to celebrate his life." I said.

Nick nods, understanding what i am saying.

"You are right, he would want you to be happy, and to only remember good times." He said.

He then gave me a gentle squeeze.

"So, are you going to the funeral, or work will be tight?" He asked.

I nod.

"I have to, it is the least I can do for him, I want to be there for my cousins and his wife. They are going to need all the support they can get." I said.

He understood my pain, he knows that losing a loved one is never easy, and he knows that my family is going to need all the help they can get.

"I will be there with you every step of the way. We will get through this together." He said.

I smiled at him and felt little better. After a difficult morning of processing the news of my uncle's death, I woke up around ten feeling bit more hopeful. I knew that the day ahead will be hard, but I was determined to get through it. With my husband by my side, I feel like I can do anything. Nick and I sent kids to school then went got ready and head to the funeral home, where we will meet the rest of the family.

We arrived there, greeted the family then went inside and greeted the rest of the family. There gave me many hugs and tears were everywhere as everyone comes together to mourn the loss. After few hours we left, and the kids were back from school. While driving we received a phone call from the babysitter, telling us that Ifalethu has come down with a fever. We increased speed.

I wonder why it is always like this, whenever something bad happened another occurs. I never get a chance to deal with one problem at the time.

As we rushed home, Ifa could sense our worry and concern. He knows that something is wrong, and he feels uneasy and unsettled. As we arrived home, we went to check on him and notice that he is burning up with fever. We gave him medication and put him to bed, hoping he will soon feel better. I felt so worried, but I tried to stay calm for the sake of my son. My poor baby is feeling miserable and uncomfortable, and all he can do is cry. He does not understand what is happening to him. We did our best to comfort him, but nothing seems to work. We spent the rest of the day taking care of him, making sure he is as comfortable as possible.

He finally fell asleep in my arms. I held him close, gently rocking him back and forth until he is completely asleep. By the end of the day, he started to feel a bit better.

I started preparing dinner just a quick thing. I called my boys; we all sat and eat. Balekile kept on telling us how horrible day because Ifa was sick. Time had come for us to tell him about Uncle Mfundo, will he even understand.

"Nana your dad and I have something to tell you." I said.

He was so heartbroken to hear about his grandfather's passing. He remembers all the fun times they shared, the laughter and the jokes, and special bond they had. Tears well up in his eyes as he thinks about how much he will miss his granddad. we console him, told him all will be fine, and it is ok to feel sad and that his grandfather would always want to see him happy and doing good at school. He nodded, trying to hold back his tears, and continued eating.

"He's in heaven right, so will he visit me whenever I ask him to?" He asked.

Nick and I looked at each other, unsure of how to answer.

"Balekile grandfather has gone to heaven, but he will always be with you in your heart." Said Nick.

"Yes, daddy is right, whenever you feel sad, he will be here to comfort you. The love between families never ends, even when someone passes away." I said.

I am sure he does not understand, he just nodded. As the evening draws closer and the sun set, we settled in for the night. After our dinner we put children into bed, read them a story and gave them goodnight kiss. Balekile held a small picture of his grandfather close to his heart and made a silent prayer for him. The house was so quiet and peaceful as we all fell asleep, as we rest to ready to face day tomorrow.

CHAPTER 41

" *A funeral is not a day in a lifetime, it is a lifetime in a day."* - David Kessler.

This quote reminds us that funerals are not just about one person's life, but about the impact they had on the people around them. A funeral is a time to celebrate the life of the person who has passed, and to support the beloved ones they left behind.

I am a strong and resilient woman. I am deeply sad by my uncle's death. But I am determined to be there for my family and to be a source of support and comfort. As the funeral service begins, I took a deep breath and prepared myself foe the emotional experience ahead. We then laid him to his final rest place.

Few months after

Our favorite couple just got married. Since this is a family dinner to celebrate a special occasion, we will want something that feels both comforting. As for food we had amazing stuff, juicy roast with roasted vegetable, creamy mashed potatoes, and gravy so delicious and mouth-watering. As for dessert, a family favourite like apple pie and chocolate cake. And don't forget the Champaign! We celebrated their love with so much affection.

I saw my husband really tried by all means to get a job, but nothing seems to happen.

It was Saturday in the afternoon, kids were Cape town with Mabusi. I was busy reading a magazine, Nick was in the garden planting some trees. I then had the idea of starting a business with him so that he can get back on his feet. I went to the garden sat down.

"I've been thinking about ways that we can increase our income while you're still looking for a full-time job. I was wondering if you'd be interested in discussing some ideas that I have." I said.

"Ok?" He said.

"Marketing agency." I said.

"And how will it work?" He said.

"I think we can start small and test the idea without a huge investment of time or money. We could create few sample products and list them for a sale on some sites. If they don't sell, we have not lost much, we can move to another idea. But if they sell, we can scale up and create more products. What do you think?" I asked.

"I hear you honey, and it sounds like a good plan." He said.

"If you have questing just ask. I just want to make sure you feel comfortable about this whole thing." I said.

Got up and let him be and contacted my lawyer about my idea. I don't know why but this guy always gets happy whenever I succeed, he like seeing me happy. One could say he loves me.

The first thing I did on Monday was to go to his office.

"So, tell me about your new idea. What type of marketing services will you be offering?" He asked.

"I am offering a full suite of marketing services is a great way to attract a wide range of clients." I said.

"What are your goals for the new business? Are you hoping to make a certain amount of money, or reach a certain number of clients?" He asked.

"Reach a certain number of clients." I said.

"That is a very realistic and attainable goal. But to reach that many clients, you will need to develop a strong marketing strategy. How do you plan to do that?"

Thet was hard to answer, perhaps I could start by developing a strong social media presence for my business, and creating engaging content that will attract new followers and clients. and I don't think there will be any problem I mean I am the face of Young Empowerment and already I have huge number of followers.

Now we got to the most important part.

"Have you decided on a business structure, like a sole proprietorship, partnership or corporation?" He asked.

Partnership." I said.

He gave papers to sign then said he will do the rest. I then went to my salon. Nobuhle was bit down, she broke up with her boyfriend and he was expecting, she had no idea how she will tell her mom, but I am here she had nothing to worry about.

Few weeks into the future, and I am sitting down with Nick, Jack and Mabusi discussing the next steps for my growing business.

"You've had a great success so far Matty, and it is clear that businesses and modelling is working, but are you prepared for the next phase of growth. Do you have any plans for expanding your team, or increasing your marketing budget?" Nick asked.

Really did not see that one coming, I couldn't answer it.

"To be honest I don't have plans yet. My focus is more on the salon and my modeling career since I am the face." I said.

Since it was already bedtime, we all went to sleep, my kids were staying with my uncle's wife, since she retired, she was being lonely plus Nokuhle is married with her kids only the last born stay there. Someone will think I cold hearted to send such small child there, but it is their own good plus I have a lot on my plate right now. One thing I am doing is for them to start being independent at such young age. Just want my kids to be as strong as their mom, nick is very weak, not that I talk ill of him, but he is my husband I know him.

Well, we slept that night, the following day I had back-to-back meetings, Nick started running the other company all by himself and I trusted him with my life. As for the modeling one I think of leaving it I am too old to be posing naked in front of other men, yeah Nick doesn't mind but what about my kids. I don't want them to be left out at school because of the work I was doing.

CHAPTER 42

*A*FTER 15 YEARS
15 years have passed, and Balekile is now a teenager in high school, while Ifalethu is in primary school. And Balekile falls in love, and I become pregnant again.

Balekile first experience with love was easy and happy. He met someone special at school and felt new from the first moment he saw her. The two of them quickly became friends and then something more. My baby had never felt so alive and happy. I was as if their whole world had opened. They knew they were in love and that it would last forever, at least that was what they were hoping for.

As months went by, Balekile's relationship with Naledi continued to grow and blossom. They promised one another heaven and earth, they told each other everything, shared their secrets and insecurities. They were so happy; they would share laugher until their sides hurt. They were the best friends as well as lovers. Until Naledi wanted to take their relationship to the next level.

"Will you be mine forever?" She asked.

Balekile's heart skipped a beat. They had never asked each other this kind of questions before, he even hesitated to answer since he did not know what to say.

"Yes, I will be." He said.

In one of those tiring days, I was coming from work I found them busy doing homework and Ifalethu was watching TV. He loves pepper pig just like his brother. When I entered the house, my baby came running to me, hugged me and helped me with my bags. I asked him to get me slippers. I had hells all day long. He rushed and got them, helped me put them on then massaged my shoulders.

"Does that feel better mama?" He said.

"Yes baby, thank you." I said.

After few minutes I got up to prepare dinner, some ingredients were missing, asked both Balekile and Naledi to get them for me and they did. I decided to cook rice, meat and mashed potatoes so Ifalethu helped me peel the potatoes while I was busy cleaning the meat. In no time they returned I started doing my mashed potatoes.

"Naledi will you be joining us for dinner?" I said.

"No, my mom asked me to help her with something." She said.

She is lying, she fears Nick. He never smiles when she is around and it's funny because he also likes her, he says she's perfect for our son. Well, Naledi left and Balekile walked her out. Went upstairs and took a shower. While showering Nick arrived from work so tired. As I relaxed in the shower, I heard the bathroom door opening and closes. The footsteps approached and then the curtain pulled back. Standing there, with smile on his face.

"Mind if I join you?" He asked.

My heart leaped with joy, and I asked him to come in. We embraced each other while the water washes over both of us as we share a tender moment together.

We got dressed and went downstairs to have dinner, everyone shared how their day was as usual, but I was feeling unwell during dinner. And I was not even sure what is wrong, but I can't shake the feeling that something is off.

We finished having food, Balekile did the dishes and Nick took Ifa to put him to sleep. While I went straight my bed and threw myself on it. Nick came sat on the study table opened his laptop and got to work. He had a very big presentation tomorrow. Only God knows when I fell asleep.

The following day I woke up, still feeling strange. Went to the rest room and got back. Sent Nobuhle messages telling her I won't come to work since I am not feeling well. I was so sweaty and feeling hot. Asked Nick to ask our neighbor to take Ifalethu since her child and Ifa attend same school, as for Balekile he said he will walk to school with Naledi. Just scared that my child does not become obsessed with this girl. Everyone left and I slept again.

A

Around 12:34 I woke up feeling even worse than I did last night and in the morning. I tried to get out of the bed but overcame with dizziness. I called my husband told him that I am not getting any better, and that I am worried something might be wrong. It is a pity because he can't come. Nick contacted the doctor and in no time he was here. Ran few tests and congratulated me. I could not follow but I was sure it has something to do with pregnancy. And yes, I was pregnant.

Surely my uncle is so annoyed because of me, I promised him that I won't make another kid, these two are fine plus the other one in heaven. The doctor gave me few meds and I felt bit better. As soon as Nick finished his work, he came straight home, came with my favorite hot wings, and gave them to me.

"You scared me, what did the doctor say?" He asked.

I took a deep breath. and looked him in the eye.

"I am pregnant." I said.

He stunned and became silent for a moment and then he laughed. He stood off the bed and started jumping up and down, singing.

"I am a father to be. I am a father to be." He said.

I laughed and took a very deep breath. I did not expect this reaction. While we were still celebrating the big news, I started to feeling bit dizzy. I sat back and relaxed.

"Maybe we should calm down a bit." I said.

Nick looked bit concerned, he sat down next to me and put him arm around me.

"Are you okay?" He said.

"I am little overwhelmed; this is such a big change." I said.

After few minutes, after we both calmed down, we were still happy and excited, but I also starting to think about what this big change will mean for our lives.

"We need to start making plans. We will need to prepare for the baby, and we will need to tell kids." He said.

I nodded and said.

"We have a lot to do." I said.

Kids arrived from school; Ifa went straight to my wings how silly. They both came to our room and greeted, Balekile is the big guy now, he does not hug nor kiss us anymore. He's always on the phone. Told them to change we are going out; I could use some fresh air. I got off the bed while we are getting ready and changed quickly.

We all got in one car and went to the mall. Went to STEARS and ordered 4 triple big bosses with cool drink, and in no time our order came, everyone had their meal. Except Balekile.

"No Balekile you have been busy since we left home, tell Naledi you'll talk to her later." I said.

"How did you know it is her." Said Nick.

"She's the only one who keeps him this busy." I said.

He put down his phone though you could see he's not happy, but he will be fine this is our time. We ate and went back home since one of us was not interested in going out with us.

CHAPTER 43

" *Family that travels together, stays together." - Unknown.*
Few weeks later it was school holidays so, we were on our way to Paris, with Naledi.

We arrived at the hotel and settle into our rooms, the boys were sharing the room with their dad, and I shared a room with Naledi, Nick and I are still young to be grandparents. The children were eager to explore the city and were also couldn't wait to. We wandered in streets of Paris, stopping at the shops and restaurants along way. You Know how children are, took pictures at the Eiffel Tower and the Louvre, and I captured every moment of our trip. We ended the day with delicious dinner. Then later Nick and I took a walk.

The next day, we visited the Palace of Versailles, explored the gardens and the royal apartments. The children kept taking pictures of everything. Nick and I told a little story about the history of the palace. After touring the palace, we decided to have lunch at a local restaurant. We enjoyed the delicious meal and then headed back to the hotel. to rest.

In the evening, we went to the top of Eiffel Tower to watch the sunset over the city. It is a magical moment, and we felt closer than ever.

My son and his girlfriend found a quite spot to share a romantic moment. They talked about their feelings for each other and how much they are enjoying their time in Paris. They then kissed, and they were so happy to have each other. Meanwhile Ifalethus explores the city with us. We visited Nitro Dame Cathedral and took a boat ride down the seine. It was a very special time for a family, and we were grateful to be together.

As for Balekile and his girlfriend, their romantic moment head back to the hotel. They felt closer than ever, and they could not stop smiling. They agreed to mee at the hotel room in few minutes. Our young couple shared a delicious meal alone and talked about their future together. They decided to make the most of their remaining time in Paris. While sharing a romantic moment thing got nasty in my room, on my bed but thankfully we didn't see it nor noticed anything. Later we all met to have dinner then went to bed. We still have more activities to do.

The next day we woke up early to visit other places. We went to the museum called Louvre, we saw the Mona Lisa and the Venus de Milo, and my kids were amazed by the art. We all spent hours wandering the museum, learning about the history of the paintings. Balekile and Naledi could not stop smiling at each other. In the afternoon we were at the hotel restaurant, so I went back to my room to put on something since I was feeling bit cold, my phone dropped, I bend down to pick it up I then saw a used Max (Condom).

I went back to them and then decided to go on a stroll. We went to Tuileries Garden and took a break for Ice cream. They children were running and playing in the park while Nick and I relaxed on a bench. later we headed back to the hotel to rest up for the evening. I asked Naledi and Balekile to come with me. We went back to my room, and I showed them what I found.

"I never did the deeds with Nick, and the room service can't just leave them here, so can anyone tell me what's going on." I said.

"Uhm mom." Said Balekile.

"You know what forget it, Naledi if you get pregnant know you two are on your own. Because you both know sex it's a bad thing for kids." I said.

Left them in the room and went back to my husband and kid. They were so scared and Naledi's eyes were teary. Balekile told her not to worry.

During dinner everyone was shocked by my announcement. those two tried to explain themselves, but I was not interested in hearing their excuses. Balekile was so worried, as for naledi she was feeling terrible for causing such big problem. They did not know how to approach me so that they could fix things. and they were worried that the family vacation is ruined.

After the final tense night at Paris, everyone packed up their belongings and went to bed. First thing in the morning everyone headed to the airport Balekile and Naledi were quite during the trip, not knowing what to say to each other or to us especially me. When, we arrived home,

Naledi apologizes to me for what happened. I accepted her apology and sent her home, but it was clear that things are not the same. As for Balekile he was not sure if i will allow his girlfriend to ever come over. Later Nick was out with his friends, Ifalethu was asleep, and I was watching TV. Balekile came and joined me.

"Mama, can I say something?" He said.

"MH." I said.

"Mom I sorry for ruining the vacation for you. You and dad needed it more than any of us. What Naledi and I did can't be undone but I am truly sorry." He said.

"I hear you baby, but what would happen if you guys made a child. You are still at school, who would look after your child, or you will drop out. And trust me no child of mine will drop out or else you will leave my house." I said.

Turned up the volume and he knew I was done talking. He went to his room and called Naledi.

"Hy sunshine." He said.

"Hey love, how's your mom?" she said.

"She is still mad. I think we should slow down things a bit. I don't want to be thrown out of the house." He said.

He made it sound as if it was a joke though I would throw him out.

"Let's hope she will be fine by tomorrow. Good night my dad is calling me." She said.

"Good night sweetie pie." He said.

After a very long tiring day, he went to sleep hoping he will talk to me again tomorrow and hoping I will be better.

The following day Nick and I were still in bed. My poor baby made coffee for us, that was nice but still acted angry so that he could see he is wrong. I had my coffee then went to shower and went to the store to check how things are going, and I got a call that I have to go to Dubai for business, from family trip to business trip, just slept home once already I am leaving again.

CHAPTER 44

" The world is a book, and those who do not travel read only one page." - Saint Augustine.

As I was preparing for a business trip, I was nervous and excited, I knew this trip could be a big opportunity for my career. I said my goodbyes to my family including Naledi, Ifalethu wished me luck and told me to have a safe trip. As I board the plane with Nobuhle, I felt hopeful and nervous.

My plane landed in Dubai, and we immediately struck by the city's beauty and energy. The hotel where we are staying was luxurious and modern. This business trip was the best out of them all. and it was important, Nobuhle and I were determined to do our best. We meet with our colleagues and get to work, but I could not stop of thinking about my kids back home.

Later we went on dinner, the colleagues shared unprofessional and inappropriate conversation. I was feeling uncomfortable, but I did not want to offend anyone. The conversation became more and more inappropriate, and I felt like I am in a difficult situation. I excused myself from the table and called Nick, told him what happened, and he sounded bit worried but i was more concerned about the voice I hear at his background.

Back in my hotel room, i was so tired from today's work. Turned off the lights and got ready for bed. I could not stop about the inappropriate conversation from the dinner. I felt uncomfortable and did not know what to do next. As I drift back off to sleep, I wonder how the rest of the business trip will go.

The thing is I am pregnant, and people were busy talking about how they don't want kids now and all that as if I made a mistake keeping this baby. And the other client kept looking me in a weird way, he even winked on me few times.

The next morning, I woke up feeling refreshed and ready to face the day. Got dressed and headed to the office, determined to put the previous night behind me. As I worked and focused on my work and tried by all mean to ignore the negative vibes. The lunch time then arrived, I had some food with the same colleagues but today they were professional and appropriate. The afternoon drew by, and it was time for me to go back to my hotel room and have medicine. On my way I received a text message from the client from the client from the previous night. IT made me uneasy and uncomfortable, so I deleted it and ignored it. I arrived at the hotel, feeling drained and overwhelmed. I took my medication and slept.

In the evening, I ordered room service and took a long hot bath, I have never felt so relived to be away from the office. As I get ready for bed, I just realised that I need to address this matter before it gets out of hands. I called the front desk and asks to speak with to a manager. the hotel manager arrived at my room and listened as I explained the situation. The manager was appalled by the client's behaviour and promises to act. I felt at ease and relived. I then went to sleep feeling safe and supported.

The following day I woke up feeling well and happy with so much strength. I headed to the office, ready to start the day. The office's atmosphere was different, and the client was nowhere to be seen. I learned that the manager took an action, and the client has been banned from the premises. I was now able to focus on my work, feeling supported and respected. Later on, I started packing. I will be leaving the first thing in the morning. Nobuhle was so busy for me since we got here. I tried inviting her to my room multiple times but no.

On the last day of the trip, I met with an important client. The client was friendly and professional, and we have a productive meeting. After meeting I took a walk around the city and just to get bit relaxed. I felt excited about leaving and I was also homesick. Later I video called nick 5 times, but he did not pick up then tried Balekile. We talked and they told me their father has not come home for 2 days now. Huh! Like how he can. I assumed the worst.

As I finished packing my suitcase, i was so mad at nick and so ready to face him. But honestly, I was so grateful for the experience I had on the trip, but I am also ready to go home. In the morning the taxi arrived, and I headed to the airport. I caught a flight and settled into my seat, thinking about all that has happened. the plane took off, and I looked out of the window. Dubai really looks great when you look at it from above.

As I arrived at the airport, I requested for uber and in no time it arrived, I went straight home worried sick about my babies and mad by their careless father. When I reached Naledi was sitting with Ifalethu outside while Balekile was watering my plants, I got out of the car and my baby came running to me, he hugged me, and I gave him million kisses. Balekile took my bags inside and I paid the uber guy.

"Why didn't you tell me you are coming, I would have come to get you." Said Balekile.

"Do you have a car?" I said.

"No, I would have come with yours." He said.

"With what license?" I said.

We laughed and got inside. I couldn't believe Nick left my kids all by themselves without saying anything. I went upstairs, took a quick shower and came to watch TV with my kids. I contacted all his friends but none of them knows where he is, including his own mom. If you can recall what Nick is doing now is what Nkosinathi did to Nandi, he also just disappeared on her but at least she was not pregnant like me, at least they had no kid.

While watching TV a message popped on my phone and it was him, he doesn't even know I am back.

"Baby I am sorry for not being able to take your calls, I was in back-to-back meetings. I hope you are enjoying Dubai; kids and I misses you and don't worry we are still ok."

CHAPTER 45

" *When you cheated on me; you cheated on us. You didn't just break my heart; you broke our future"* - *Steve Maraboli*

It is complicated and sensitive situation, so I will try to treat it carefully. I think the most important thing is to communicate with Nick when he gets here, and I hope whatever kept him away from his kids is important. Cheating can be really Damaging to a relationship, and it is important to acknowledge that. As one it is important to try to understand why you have been cheated at. There might be issues that need to be addressed.

Moreover, it is important for both people to take responsibility for their actions. The one who cheated should take responsibility for their choices, and the person who was cheated at should try to heal without drama being caused. It is not an easy road, but it is worth.

Later when Nick walked in the door, I was angry, sad and relieved that he is not hurt. I wanted to confront him, but I also felt like I just have to pretend as if everything is fine and wait for the right time. I am afraid of what might happen if I confront him, but I might also be afraid of what will happen if I don't.

I got up from the couch and went to the kitchen, he was so shocked to see me. He greeted and crabbed me from behind, but I was so serious I couldn't pretend. I left him standing all alone in the middle of the kitchen. Balekile could sense tension between us, he took his baby brother and went upstairs to play Tv games.

I went upstairs and he followed me, trying to talk to me but I kept ignoring him. I didn't want to talk to him, and it was clear on my face, he went on the bathroom to take a shower. The message pop up on his phone that says.

"Thanks for the great night! can't wait to see you again soon."

My heart torn into many pieces, and I felt like I am going to throw up. I felt betrayed and angry. When he got out the shower, he saw his phone on my hand tears falling like a rain. He was shocked to see me holding his phone, and he knew he has been caught. He was feeling defensive and ashamed. I was so furious and hurt and I demanded an explanation. I wanted to know who the text was from and for how long it has been going on.

"Can you please tell me who pumpkin is?' I said.

"Baby it's not how it looks." He said.

"You know what don't bother, I guess she is more important than your kids, she's worth your time, hence you decided to leave your kids all by themselves for 3 days, whole 3 days. You know what get all your things and get out of my house, I never want to see you near this house or my kids Never." I said.

"Baby please let me explain. I didn't mean to." He said.

"You said the same thing last time." I said.

"We can still fix this baby, please." He said.

"When you cheated on me, you cheated on us. You didn't just break my heart; you broke our future." I said.

And I was done talking, I took my phone and waited for him outside.

Sorry to say this but he was nothing in the last 15 years, I loved him regardless of being jobless I even started a company just for him, but he will know who I am.

He took all his things when he was about to take the car keys I stood up.

"You better leave my car keys, that car was brought with my money, you can ask pumpkin to buy you one." I said.

"Baby please don't be like this." He said.

"Nick get out of my house and please leave the house keys behind you won't need them anymore." I said.

I went to open the door for him since it seemed like he forgot how it works. He left with shame, and I did not care.

I sat alone in my bedroom, my emotions trigged. I felt so betrayed and angry, but also lost and confused. Since it's still holidays, I'll send my kids at Mabusi's don't want them to see me in pain. The following day I packed their bags and they left though Balekile did not want to, but he eventually understood me for the sake of his baby brother.

This is mature and selfless decision on my part. My children are my top priority, even in the mist of all this pain. Sending my babies away also gave me some space to really process the emotions and figure out what to do next.

Days went by but I couldn't get any better, I have reached my breaking point, and I can't forgive Nick for his actions. So, I decided to move on and start afresh. That is a big decision I know but it might be the best one for me and for the sake of my peace.

Divorce is a difficult process, but it might be the best way for me to heal and move forward.

Around 12:30 I got ready and went to the office and called Nick in my office. I told him that I can't work with him anymore, and that he needs to pack his things and leave. He was shocked and tried to ague, but I did not want to hear anything. he left the office confused and lost. I took a deep breath and started to clean up my desk. I knew it is going to be a long road ahead, but I am determined to make it work.

Later I called a divorce lawyer and set up a meeting. The lawyer asked me about the situation, and I explained what happened. The lawyer was sympathetic and offered advice on how to move forward. We discussed the assets and how they should divide. The lawyer told me that it is important to be organized and to keep records of everything. I was a relief to have someone on my side.

CHAPTER 46

" *D*ivorce isn't such a tragedy. a tragedy's staying in an unhappy marriage, teaching your children the wrong things about love. Nobody ever dies of divorce." - Jennifer Weiner.

Nick was shocked when he receives the divorce papers. He cannot believe that our marriage is over. He was felled with regrets and sadness, and he was angry at himself.

He thought back on all the moments we shared, the good times and the bad. He wanted to fix this so badly, but it was too late. As he reflects on the past, he realises that he made mistakes. He wished he had been more faithful and had control to his needs and desires. He picked up his phone and called me hoping I will answer. When I did, he tried apologizing, but I was not ready to listen. I Hanged up the phone.

He thinks back on all the moments we shared, the good times and the bad. He wonders what he could have done differently. As he reflects on the past, he realizes that he made mistakes. He wishes he had been more attentive to my needs and more willing to compromise. He wants to try to make things right, but he doesn't know if it's too late. He picks up the phone and called me hoping I'll answer. When I did, he tried to apologize, but I was not ready to listen. I hung up the phone, and he felt more lost than ever.

Meanwhile I was at work trying to focus but I can't stop thinking about the divorce papers and what the future holds. I felt anger, sadness and even a bit of relief. At lunchtime, I went for a walk trying to clear my head. As I was walking, I saw a little girl playing in the park, and it made me think of my childhood. I started feeling bit down and missed my parents. I really wondered if I made a right decision. Back at the Office, I tried to refocus on my work, but it was still hard to concentrate. My thoughts kept drifting to Nick and the life we had together. I thought about our wedding day and the years that followed. I felt like our marriage was a dream that turned into a nightmare. I started to think about what I will do next, and whether I will ever be able to trust again.

As for my poor babies, Ifalethu is still young, he can't understand everything. My sweet and sensitive Balekile is having a hard time. He loves us both and does not want us separate. he tries to act like everything is normal, but it is not working. His grandmother told me he is having trouble of sleeping, he is always quiet and distant. He just wants everything to go back to the way it was before.

The following day:

I was feeling physically fit and healthy. My pregnancy is going smoothly, and I feel more energized than before. I just loved the feeling when the baby moves or kick, and I can't wait to hold my baby. I had already picked few names and decorated the nursery. As I sit in the waiting room at the doctor's office, the feeling of coming to know by baby's gender made me so excited.

In the doctor's office:

I had few check-ups, everything looked great, and the doctor gave me a clean bill of health. I asked the doctor about what to expect in the third trimester, and the doctor provided some health advice. On the way out of the office, i saw a couple in the waiting room, The woman was pregnant, and the man was rubbing her back and looking at her with such love. i felt so sad and wish Nick was there with me.

After the doctor's appointment, I was driving home when I saw a sign for a park. I decided to stop for few minutes to clear my head. as I walk through the park, I heard children laughing and playing on swings. The sight of the children made me think of the child i am carrying, started feeling emotional. A kind stranger asked if I was okay, tears started skipping to my cheeks.

The stranger offered me a tissue and a hug. He told me that everything will be okay. I started to feel a little better. without knowing the stranger, I trusted him and told him everything, and he offered me words of wisdom and encouragement. Started to feel a more hopeful and i decided to head home.

Later I went to see my babies and they were happy to see me and wanted to come back home, but I promised to take them on Friday. Told the older baby to take a very good care of his baby brother and he promised to. I then left and went straight home and thrown myself on the bed; I was so tired after this long tiring day. As I lied on bed, I could not stop thinking about the kind stranger. I closed my eyes and saw the man's face. I wonder who the man is and if he has a family. I immediately felt guilty for thinking about him, but I can't stop. The thoughts kept me up all night.

The next day, I decided to head to the mall to run few errors and get some groceries since my kids are coming back tomorrow. As I was walking through the mall, I saw someone who looked familiar. It is the same man from the park! I was surprised and curious. The man walked up to me and said.

"Hi, I am so glad to see you again." He said.

I was at loss of words but talked to him eventually.

"Oh hi, I am so sorry. I'm little surprised to see you here. I did not expect to run into you again." I said.

He smiled and said.

"I know it's a coincidence, but I am glad it happened. I wanted to thank you for being so open and talking to me yesterday. It meant a lot." He said.

I was touched by his sincerity.

"Do you mind if I ask what you were doing in park yesterday?" I said.

The man nodded and said.

"I was walking my dog. He gets so excited when he gets to go to the park. He is like a big kid. What about you? What brings you to the mall today?" He asked.

"I was just running some errands, but now that we are here, maybe we could get a coffee or something? I'd love to get to know you better." I said.

The man agreed and we head to the food court for a cup of coffee. We chatted about our lives, our families and our hopes and dreams. We really have a lot in common. As I finished my coffee, I realised it is getting late and I need to get back to my errands. I thanked him for the coffee and conversation. he then said.

"I really enjoyed talking to you. If you ever want to talk again here is my number." He said.

he handed, me a piece of paper with his number on it. I smiled and put the paper in my purse. as I waked away, I felt a flutter in my stomach.

CHAPTER 47

" If the person you love doesn't love your back, let them go. They are not the right person for you, and you will find someone else. Don't be afraid to let love to visit again. - Henry David Thoreau.

I headed to the store, but my thoughts kept drifting to the man at the mall or should I say the park? When I got home, I put the groceries away and sat down in the couch. I took out the paper with the number out of my purse. I could not decide whether to call him or not. After some time, I decided to take time to think things over before calling the man. I want to be sure that my feelings are genuine, and not just the results of a chance encounter at the mall. I don't want it to be seen as if I am using the man to heal. I did my daily routines, but my thoughts kept going back to the man. I can't stop wondering what the man must be doing.

As I got ready for bed, I thought about how my life is about to change. I tried to focus on the task ahead- the court date the next day – but I can't help it but think about the man at the mall. I finally got to sleep, still unsure of the future and what will happen to me and my children, especially the unborn one. As I slept, I dreamed of a bright and hopeful future. The next day, I woke up feeling refreshed and determined. I took a quick bath and wore casual clothes and headed to the court. I was really nervous, but I know that I am doing the right thing. When I arrived at the courthouse, I took a deep breath and got inside. I was called into the courtroom and took a seat. The judge asked me some questions and I answered honestly. The judge looked at me and said.

"I understand this is a difficult time for you, especially when you are pregnant. But I am confident that you're making the right decision." He said.

I felt bit relieved and nervous. As I left the courtroom, Nick was called in. He sat down and looked nervous. The judge asked him some questions and his answers were hesitant and uncertain. The judge can tell that he was not ready to let go of this marriage. He looked at Nick and said.

"I know this is hard, but it is time to move on. You need to accept that this relationship is over and focus on your future." He said

Nick was sad and angry, but he knew a this is on him.

The judge then called me inside. He looked at both of us and took a deep breath.

"I see that there is still some unresolved tension between you two. I think it would be best if you both had some time to talk through your issues in mediation." He said.

We looked at each other and nodded. We went to a small room with a mediator and began to talk through our problems. Nick and I sat down with the mediator and began to talk. We shared our feelings and our thoughts, and the mediator helped us to see each other's point of view.

"I know that we had good time, but I just don't think we were right for each other anymore." I said.

"I understand that, and I know that I made some mistakes. I just want to make things right. Only if you let Mr." He said.

I looked after him, looked away and took a deep breath.

After a few more sessions with the mediator, we had reached an understanding and our limits. We agreed to put our differences aside and focus on co-parenting our kids. We were both committed to making sure that our children are well taken care of and happy. But Nick was still sad and had a huge regret, but we were slowly starting to move in.

Weeks went by since my babies had come back home. As for their grandmother she started acting weird towards me. Since the divorce was settled Nick got nothing from it. But I was happy with my kids, not to forget the man from the mall Sibongile Xaba that was his name. We have been seeing each other and he's ok with my pregnancy and my kids love him. Nick was so furious when he found out that I had started seeing someone new. He feels like I have moved on too quickly and that I don't care about the kid's well-being. He felt like I was being selfish, and I was only thinking about myself.

Since I was the one who asked for a divorce, he also decided to file a lawsuit against me. That created even more tension and conflict between us, and it made it even harder for us to co-parent and it is also possible that the lawsuit would be successful, since I had a legitimate reason to fire him.

One day, he received a phone call from Balekile's school. My child had been acting out in class and has been disruptive. The school counselor suggested that he might be struggling with the divorce and that it would be helpful for him to talk to a therapist. Nick felt guilty and angry that I was not able to take that ca when they were calling me. He agreed to take him to the therapist. I really wonder with what money because he doesn't have a job. He called me and asked to meet with me in person. I asked Sibongile to come with me since I don't know what Nick will do. When we met,

"I can't believe that you have started seeing someone new. Don't want care about how this will affect our children?" He asked.

"I am not trying to hurt anyone, but I need to move on with my life. I can't stay stuck in the past." I said.

He was so angry but tried by all means to control his emotions.

"You will regret this." He said.

"Did you call me here to tell me that?" I said.

He looked at Sibongile and shake his head.

"No, you can leave." He said.

He then left us standing there, I knew he was planning something. We also left. When I reached home Ifalethu was already at home from school. He came running to me with tears in his eyes.

"Baby what's wrong." I said.

"Balekile locked himself in the room, he won't let me in. and I heard him screaming." He said.

I quickly went inside to check on my baby. I knocked at his door, but he won't open. I went downstairs and sent Ifalethu to play, I wiped his tears and kissed him on his forehead.

"Do you want me to check up on him?" said Sibongile.

"No, let's give him some space he will come around. And sorry for getting you caught in all of this." I said.

"No don't be, I understand." He said.

He hugged me and I felt safe in his arms but to be honest I am afraid our relationship will end up like mine and Nick's. And I am worried about Balekile. This whole thing is going to destroy my baby if I don't act soon.

CHAPTER 48

" *Motherhood can be selflessness and difficult, but the joy and fulfilment that it can bring it's priceless."*

As a mother I had to act, I took Balekile to a therapist. As he started therapy, Balekile learned new ways to cope with divorce. He started being more hopeful. He learned that us divorcing was not his fault and it will never be. Balekile also learned that it is important to focus on his own well-being.

One day we were just sitting watching TV.

"How are you feeling lately? Has therapy been helping?" I asked.

"I am feeling sad sometimes, but I'm starting to feel a little 8. It helped talking to someone who understands what I am going through." He said.

"I am glad to hear that. You know you can always talk to me if you need to." I said.

He smiled and nodded and said.

"Thank you, mom. I really appreciate that." He said.

"How is Naledi, how are things going?" I asked.

"It's been a little awkward, but we are still friends. I think it is going to take some time to adjust to everything." He said.

"that's totally understandable. You don't worry about rushing anything. Just take things in your own pace." He said.

He nodded.

"That really means a lot to me. Thanks." He said.

The following day I went to work and found papers from Nick's lawyer regarding the unfair dismissal case. The case was going to take place the day after. As I read the papers, I felt so anxious. I know that the case would have a big impact on my children's, and I was worried about what would happen. I know that I need to be strong for my kids, but I can't help feeling scared and uncomfortable. The day went by with stress and all.

The next day, I went to work to do a few things, then to the court. In the courtroom, Nick's lawyer argues that I had no legal grounds to fire him, and that Nick was unfairly dismissed. My lawyer argues that Nick's infidelity was a clear violation of the company's code of conduct, and that his actions were not right for the company. The judge listened to both sides, and then decided.

The judge ruled in my favor. He explained that Nick's infidelity was a clear violation of the company's code of conduct, and that Nick's infidelity was not right for the company. The judge also noted that the kid's well-being should be a top priority for both parents. Nick was disappointed by the judge's decision, but he knew he had to accept it.

We were both frustrated and angry. Nick and his mom felt like he was unfairly treated, and I felt like Nick was not ready to give up on this matter. The tension between us turned into hatred. Balekile on the other hand just wants everyone to get along, but he doesn't know how to make that happen.

Finally, he decided to take a step back and let the adults figure things out on their own. My baby then focused on his schoolwork and the things that make him happy, like spending time with friends and playing sports. He knows that we will work things out eventually and can't control what happens. At the end he felt peaceful and calm, even though the situation was still stressful.

The therapist has been a real help for his process the divorce and the emotions that come with it. He has learned some new coping skills, and he is starting to feel more confident with more self-esteem. The therapist was impressed with his progress.

Later we were having dinner with Naledi and her parents. They told us they are moving to a different state. Both Naledi and Balekile were devastated and heartbroken. As we all know distance relationships have their own people and some are not able to control themselves when there are apartments their partners. As for Naledi, she was not happy with her parent's decision. She can't understand why her parents would make this decision to take her away.

"I don't want to leave. I am really upset and scared about what will happen if we move. I have lived here my whole life. Please don't make me go" Said Naledi.

Her parents were so sad to see their child sad. But they felt like moving is necessary for the family. Naledi's parents try to reassure her that everything will be okay, and she will visit Balekile every holiday, but she is not convinced.

After several days of arguing, Naledi's parents can see how upset she is. Like parents they decided to sit down with her and have an open and honest conversation about moving to another city. They explained why going away was so important and they wanted her to see how this would be a huge advantage for her to get a better education. She was still upset, but she started to understand why they were moving away. Her parents promised to make sure she could stay in touch with Balekile, and they offered some ideas about how she can cope with the change.

As for my son, he was not ok at all. He just fought the divorce depression now this. In the afternoon they met to talk about this, Naledi could see Balekile was not ok.

"I know this is hard for you to accept. I'm sorry that my parents are making us move. I want you to know that I'll be your girlfriend, no matter what. I will make sure we stay connected, even if we are far away. I hope you can understand why we have to move, but I'm starting for you, no matter what." She said.

He was moved by Naledi's words and started to feel a little better. He looked at her and said.

"I know you are trying to help, but I am still so sad about this. I feel like my whole world is falling apart." He said.

Naledi put her arm around his shoulder and took a deep breath.

"I know if feels like that right now, but I promise it won't always feel this way. Change is hard, but it can also be an opportunity for new and I can get the best education ever. I know it is hard to see that right now, but I really think it is for the best. Plus, I will be visiting you every holiday." She said.

A tear escaped from Balekile's eyes. And Naledi held his hands.

"I love you Naledi." He said.

"I love you too." She said.

They hugged and Balekile walked Naledi to her place.

CHAPTER 49

" *Once you are a mom, you are a mom. It's like riding a bike. you never forget." - Halle Berry.*

He got in the house, and he found me helping Ifalethu with his homework. His eyes were red, I could see he had been crying. I asked him to sit beside me.

"I know how hard this is for you. I want you to know that I'm and for you, and I am going to do everything I can to help you through this. I also want you to know that your girlfriend really cares about you. She's been very upset about this move too; I mean you saw how she fought her parents. She really loves you and she does not want to lose you and wants to stay connected with you. I hope you can feel that, even though it's right now." I said.

He smiled at me, kissed me on my cheek and went to his room.

After a few months.

I had settled into a new routine. My children were doing well at school, Balekile and Naledi were still in touch and talking every day. Everything is starting to feel like is getting back on track. I am so grateful for Sibongile, who has been a source of support through this difficult time. I started to feel like my old self again.

I noticed that I now love Sibongile, I no longer like him. I enjoy spending time with him. As for my other company I started facing losses due to the divorce and I let it shut down since it only remains me of Nick. But my salon was doing perfectly fine. Oh, I forgot to mention I have been replaced aa the Face of Young Empowerment since I am pregnant, and they made my work easier.

Someday me and Sibongile headed to the doctor's office together since I never spoke to Nick in a very long time. He does not even call to ask about his kids. I was feeling a little nervous, but also excited. The doctor called us in, and we sat down. He then said.

"I am glad you could both make it. I wanted to tell you about the results of the prenatal tests we did. "He said.

His assistant handed us a piece of paper with the results. He told us that the results of the tests are good. The baby is developing normally and there are no signs of any problems. I was so happy about that. I hugged Sibongile and smiled. The doctor congratulated me and said I should enjoy the rest of my pregnancy.

My babies, Sibongile and I spent the next few weeks preparing for the baby's arrival. We chose few names for the baby, Ifalethu and Balekile decorated the nursery, and I bought all the things the baby will need. I was so excited and nervous, but also looking forward to becoming a parent to my baby girl. Finally, the big day arrived.

I woke up in the middle of the night, I was feeling a sharp pain in my stomach. I sat up straight and the pain became worse. I realized that my water has broken, and I need to get to the hospital. I took my phone and called Balekile, he came running to my room. He called for an ambulance. As we were waiting for the ambulance to arrive. My pain got stronger and stronger. Balekile packed all needed things for the baby and me. The ambulance finally arrived, and I was rushed to the hospital. While Balekile looked after his brother and called his dad to tell him, he couldn't reach him. Disappointing as usual.

When I arrived at the hospital, I was taken to the delivery room. The doctor and nurses prepared me for the birth, and they told me what to expect. I mean hello I'm mother of 2 already. The labor was long and hard, but I was determined to get through it. I don't know when Sibongile got here but he was by my side the whole time, offering encouragement and support. Finally, after hours of labor, the baby was born.

I finally met my baby girl. Later I went home. Everyone took turns holding the baby and gazing at the baby's little face. They can't the that the baby is finally here. The baby was healthy and perfect I'm every way. I was exhausted, but I was filled with love for my new baby. I was disappointed that Nick was not there. As for Mabusi she only asked for the picture of the baby from Balekile. She really distanced herself from me.

After some time, I was sitting on the bed, Balekile and Ifalethu got in and sat with me. Ifalethu was so curious about the baby.

"Your new baby sister is so cute right? I know you are going to love her." I said.

"Can I hold her." Said Ifalethu.

"Of course, you can. But please be very careful, she is tiny." I said.

He gently held the baby and looked at her with a smile, I think they will get along very well.

"What is her name?" asked Balekile.

"I haven't named her yet, I am still trying to decide a sweet, better name for her, but I'll decide soon." I said.

My children were so excited to have a new baby sister. The next few days were bit tough as I now have to look after the baby, the house chores and the business. But at least after school two brothers would help here and there, they even learned how to feed, change and soothe the baby. These days the house is filled with joy as we all adjusted to life with a newborn, the baby was growing and changing every day. My children loved helping with the baby, even if it meant changing dirty diapers. The baby was the center of attention, and as for Ifalethu he was happy to have a new playmate.

CHAPTER 50

*O*ne morning we were having breakfast. My baby girl was still asleep, she has to I didn't sleep the whole night.

Balekile decided to make sandwiches for everyone while having breakfast someone knocked at the door. Ifalethu went to open it.

"Daddy!" he said.

"Hi, champ how are you?" He said.

"I am fine, mommy has a new baby. And it's a girl. Do you want to play with us?" He said.

My poor baby thought his father would agree but he disappoints all the time. But he still hopes that one day he will do the right thing.

"Not today. I want to see the baby." He said.

"I'm not sure that's a good idea." I said

"I'm the baby's father. I have a right to see her." He said.

"And I'm the baby's mother, you can't just walk in my house and tell us you want to see the baby. Just come another time and don't forget to call before budging in my house like that." I said.

He started shouting.

"Matty! I want to see my child." He said.

"Mzwandile, I said no. Lower your voice you will wake the baby." I said.

He did not listen he went upstairs and went straight to my room. He found her sleeping so peacefully. His eyes became teary realizing how he messed up. He lifted her and walked around the room singing lullaby. I walked in and saw they were bonding, I let them be.

"Mom, do you want me to go and talk to dad." Said Balekile.

"No baby this is between adults." I said.

"But are you ok?" He said.

"Yeah, I'm fine." I said.

We carried on having breakfast, in a few minutes he came downstairs and stood by the door looked at me and left. I knew he was angry, and he was going to do something for sure. After Breakfast Balekile did the dishes, Ifalethu packed the toys in the box, and I cleaned here and there. While cleaning we got another visitor, Nobuhle. She had baby clothes in her hands. I guess she came to brag that she is still with her baby daddy and I'm not. I wonder what went wrong between us or if my success is a burden to them who knows. I make them shake whenever I appear.

We offered her something to drink but she was in a hurry. Since Nick left, I have been feeling really weird. It feels like something bad is going to happen. Around 12:50 I asked Balekile to go to the mall to get few things for the baby. My baby has a driver's license. How cute, but he can't drive because I don't have a car anymore but not for long my name is Matty.

As I was sitting watching TV, Ifalethu was playing with the baby next to me and Sibongile arrived. I got up and hugged him. Ifalethu loves him a lot, he always comes with sweets for him. We sat down.

"How are you sweetheart? And how did you sleep?" He said.

"I'm OK and I didn't sleep. Our girl here was awake the whole night. How was your day?" I said.

"Hectic but great." He said.

"Nick was here to meet the child." I said

"Ok." He said.

That was not the answer I expected but what can he say. The feeling kept coming.

"I have been feeling weird since He left." I said.

"What feeling?" He said.

"Don't know really but it's like something bad is going to happen." I said.

"No man you're just thinking too much. Where's Balekile." He said.

"I sent him to the mall." I said.

While watching TV my phone rang and I saw the caller ID was from the salon. I answered the phone and heard a loud voice on the other end.

"Ms. Matty, there's been an accident at the salon! The building is on fire." Said the lady.

My heart started racing and I felt sick in my stomach.

"Is everyone okay?" I asked.

The lady took a very deep breath, I could sense something is wrong.

"I don't know, but the fire department is on the way." She said.

I hung up the phone and looked at Sibongile and he looked back.

"I have to go, there's been an accident at my salon." I said.

While I was upstairs changing. Balekile arrived and Sibongile told him I said there's an accident at the salon. They were scared, Balekile looked after the kids and Sibongile came with me. I got in the car; he drove to the salon as fast as he can. The closer we get to the salon, the more smoke we see in the air. My heart was broken, as we pulled up to the salon. I saw my entire building was covered in flames. I jumped out of the car and ran towards the building. I could not believe what I'm seeing.

Just as I was still trying to find out what happened to my salon, my phone rang again. I answered the phone and heard a calm voice on the other end,

"Mrs. Jackson, this is Detective Jones from the police department. I need to ask you some questions." She said.

My heart dropped as I realized what the phone ca was about.

"Do you know anyone who would want to hurt you and your family." She said.

I went deep on my thoughts for a moment and then said.

"Yes, my ex-husband." I said.

"What makes you say that?" she said.

I told the detective about Nick's history of anger and bad behavior. I told the detective about the last time Nick was at the salon, and how he threatened me.

"I'm going to need to ask you to come down to the station to make a statement." She said.

I agreed to go to the station. As I hung up the phone, I had a fear and anger. I know that I will have to be strong to get through this. We went down to the police station and met the detective.

CHAPTER 51

" Some days are just a living hell. But then there's tomorrow, which is always a fresh new start." - Lauren Graham.

At the police station, I was rushed into an interrogation room. The detective sat across from me and said,

"Mrs Jackson, we…." She said

I interpreted.

"Ms Gumede or Matty." I said.

"Oh, sorry Matty we need to ask you some questions about your ex-husband and the fire at your salon." She said.

I took a deep breath and prepared myself for what may come. The detective asked.

"Did your ex-husband ever make specific threats against you or your salon?" she asked.

I thought back too many times Nick was angry with me for working long hours at the salon.

"No, but he always made it clear that he didn't like that I worked there." I said.

The detective nodded, wrote something down and then said.

"What about other people did your ex-husband have any grudges against other people at the salon?" she said.

I thought about all the stylists and assistants who worked at the salon, but none has ever complained about him, in fact they all loved him.

"No, I don't so." I said.

She thanked me for my time and said.

"We will be in touch if we have any more questions. In the meantime, I want you to be careful and make sure you have someone with you at all times." she said.

I left the station and felt so scared, but and so unease. I know that the situation is far from over. As we drove home, I thought of how my salon caught fire, who could be behind this if it was done on purpose. We reached home, my bay was asleep, his brother is doing a very good job. I told him what happened at the salon and police station. Even mentioned that I suspect his dad.

"No mama do what you have to be. If dad did this, he is wrong and he has to be punished so don't worry about us." He said.

Hearing him saying all that made my heart be at ease. It was already late, I started preparing dinner.

"Are you joining us?" I asked.

"Uhm no, I have to be somewhere, you know how it's like being a vet. It's hectic. Oh, look at the time, I'm late already bye sweetheart." Said Sibongile.

"Ok bye." I said.

He kissed me on the cheek and left. He has started behaving weirdly and jumpy lately especially when his phone rings. Maybe it's work. I cooked, bathed my baby girl, and dished for everyone. We all ate and went to sleep.

The police kept on with the investigation about the fire, and the found some evidence against Nick. He got arrested and charged. He pleaded not guilty, but the evidence against him is strong. The trial began, and I was called to testify. I took the stand and told the court everything I know about the fire and my ex-husband's behaviour leading up to it. The trial went on for weeks, and I started feel drained and exhausted. But I knew that I am doing the right thing by making Nick pay for his bad deeds.

Though getting Nick arrested will be a good punishment for him, it won't rebuild my salon and my kids will be the ones to suffer so I decided to drop the charges against him. Some people think I did the right thing by moving on with my life. Others think that I am making a mistake by not holding Nick accountable. But I know that this is the right decision for me. Even though he will not be facing any legal consequences, I feel like a weight has been lifted off my shoulders.

Few weeks after, my salon was rebuilt. Luckily, I had it insured. Everything went back to normal but as for Sibongile he has been too busy for me lately. He even goes days without talking to me nor call or text.

It was on Saturday in the afternoon, Naledi had visited us plus she wanted to meet the baby, so her parents sent her over for the weekend. I was watering my front trees; kids were inside the house playing with our little doll. We haven't named her yet. A car pulled over my house it was Sibongile and the other lady. He seemed so scared, they got off the car and approached me.

"Hello, can we please talk to Matty." Said the Lady.

"I am Matty." I said

Looked at Sibongile really confused and looked at the lady again.

"Can we go inside and talk." She said.

"This is really not necessary." Said Sibongile

"Yeah, sure come in." I said

I was so confused by Sibongile's behaviour as if we don't know each. We got inside sent the kids upstairs and we sat down.

"You have a really beautiful house." she said.

"Thank you. Uhm, I don't know if I'm being forward, but do we know each other?" I asked.

"No, but you know my husband." she said.

"Your husband?" I asked.

"Yes, I'm Mrs Xaba, Sibongile is my husband." She said.

I looked at him and he looked away. I was shocked to know that Sibongile is married. I felt betrayed and hurt, but also confused. I had no idea that the man was married, and I had developed real feelings for him. I wonder if he had been lying to me from the start, or what. I didn't know what to believe.

"What, married, Sibongile. Wait wait wait. Are you married?" I asked.

He looked at the table and said.

"Yes, I am. I'm sorry Matty. I should have told you from the start." he said.

I was so heartbroken and Furious.

"Why didn't you tell me? Did you ever care about me at all?" I asked.

He looked at his wife and said.

"Of course, I cared about you, and I still do. But I was afraid to tell you the truth. I know that what I did was wrong, and I'm sorry." He said.

I was not sure what to think. His apology seems sincere, but I feel so hurt and betrayed.

"I need some time to think about all of this. I don't know if I can ever forgive you but what I'm sure about is that it's over between us." I said.

"I understand. I am so sorry again and I love you Matty, yes, I do." He said.

I looked at him then his wife and his wife were also looking at him. I got up and asked them to leave. His wife got out, he tried holding my hand, but I pushed him, and he left.

CHAPTER 52

" *A* new relationship is like a new house. In the beginning, it's all shiny and perfect but eventually you have to live in it day after day and then it's not so new and you realize it has flaws and maybe isn't perfect but it's your home." - Susane Colasanti.

Later I was in my room trying to put my baby to bed, message popped on my phone it was from Sibongile.

"I know I have hurt you and I am so sorry. I have been trying to figure out why I did what I did. I have come to realize that I have been unhappy in my marriage for a long time. I was looking for something that I wasn't getting from my wife. I know that I do not have to excuse what I did, but I wanted you to know why. I never meant to hurt you." He said.

My heart started beating so fast, I then fell on the floor. Luckily Ifalethu was coming to my room to check up on the baby. He saw me lying there, called his brother and called an ambulance. It took time so Balekile to my car keys and took me to the hospital. Naledi stayed with Ifalethu and the kid.

At the hospital, they put me in a coma and the doctors began to run tests. My heart was racing, and I am having difficulty breathing. The doctors were trying to figure out what's wrong and how to help me. In the waiting room, Balekile was looking down saying a little prayer and Sibongile was pacing back and forth, clearly worried and upset. He looked at his phone and saw the last message he sent to me. He thought about what he said and regretted it.

They were waiting for news about my condition, he thinks about his marriage and how unhappy he has been. He realizes that he has been taking me for granted and that he has not been the right man he should have been for me. He thinks about how his actions have affected me and how much he has hurt me. He knows that he needs to make things right, no matter what happens to me. Suddenly, a nurse came out of the room and approached them.

He looked at Balekile and Sibongile and said.

"She is stable, and she will be OK. The doctors were able to treat her heart condition and she is now resting. She will need some time to recover, but she's will to be fine." Said the nurse.

Sibongile was relieved and happy that I am Ok. He had started beating himself up for my condition. He thanked the nurse, asked Balekile to go home and look after the kids. He then came in my wars. I was still asleep, Sibongile took my hand and sat by my side. In sometimes I woke up and saw him by my side. At first, I was confused, but then I remembered everything that had happened. I started crying and said.

"I can't believe you are here after all that you put me through. I thought I'd never see you again." I said.

He took my hand and said.

"I am so sorry for everything. I have been a terrible man and a terrible person. I know that I have hurt you and I will never be able to make that right. But I want to try to make things better. I want to make you happy, if you will let me." He said.

"But you are married to Sibongile, your wife is at home, waiting for her husband to come which is you. I know that you have feelings for me, and if they are there for real, but you also have responsibilities to her. You need to accept that there's no way forward." I said.

He looked down at his hands and said.

"I know I have been wrestling with this for a long time. I don't know what to do really." He said

I put my hand on his and said.

"I think you know what to do. You just don't want to admit it to yourself. Male a decision Sibongile and stop toying with our lives." I said.

He looked at me and asked.

"What do you mean?" He asked.

"I think you know that you need to end things with me. You need to go back to your wife and focus on your marriage. It's not fair to string me along while you try to figure out what you want." I said.

"You are right. I have been selfish and unfair to both of you. I need to make things right." He said.

"I know it's hard. But it's the right thing to do." I said.

He left the room, and I was left alone with my thoughts. I felt so bad after all that. I wonder if I did the right thing by pushing him to make a decision. I also wonder if I will ever see him again. I feel a sense of loss, but also feel like a weight has been lifted off my shoulders.

The following day I got discharged. My babies were worried sick about me. Balekile came to get me, when I reached home food was already on the table only waiting to be ate up. I lifted my baby and kissed her, not to forget the older one. We had our food, and I went upstairs to rest.

Sibongile's wife got a shocking call from Sibongile's lawyer, telling her that he has filed for divorce. She was surprised, but not entirely shocked. Their divorce took place without anything disturbing. But as for the wife nothing was make sure. She made it clear that Sibongile won't be happy if he leaves her.

One day I was surprised to receive a message from Sibongile. The message simply said,

"I miss you and I divorced my wife.

I didn't know how to respond. Part of me wanted to tell him that I miss him too, but I also think that is probably not a good. I thought about all the reasons why I shouldn't. Also thought about how much I care for him and how much he means to me. Finally, I decided to reply.

"I am really sorry to hear about your divorce. Can you tell me what happened.!" I said.

A few minutes later, he replied.

"I just realized that I wasn't happy in my marriage. I wanted more out of life, and I realized that I couldn't get that with my wife. I am not trying to blame her, but I just knew that we weren't right for each other." he said

I became quiet for a moment, then I replied.

"I understand, but why are you texting me now after all this time?" I asked.

"I know that it's probably weird to hear from me after all this time. But I wanted you to know that I'm not holding on to the past. I'm trying to move forward and live my life in a way that makes me happy. I thought you deserved to know that." He said.

I was touched by his message. I know that it was hard for him to reach out, and I appreciate his honesty.

"Thank you for telling me this. I'm I that you are happy. I hope you find everything you're looking for." I said.

NEW MATTY NEW JOURNEY

"The journey of a thousand miles begins with one step." - Lao Tzu.

CHAPTER 53

" *G*rief is in two parts. The first is loss. The second is the remaking of life." - *Anne Roiphe.*

After a few days, I started to feel like I should have said something else. Something that would have let Sibongile know that I still care about him, even if we can't be together. But then I remembered myself that it's probably best to leave the past in the past.

After thinking about it for a few days, I then decided to text him.

"I just wanted to say that I hope you're well. I know that it must have been hard to go through a divorce, but I know you're strong and you'll come out of this even stronger. I wish you all the best." I said.

Few hours he replied.

"Thank you so much. It really means a lot to hear from you. I appreciate your kind words. I hope you are doing well too." He said.

We are separated by circumstances beyond our control. We now live in a different society. We know that our love is forbidden, but we can't help the way we feel. We try by all means to stay away from each other, but we just can. We still check up on each other. Finally, we decided to try and see where it goes. We have secret meetings and stolen moments, but we know that it can't last.

Should we continue to pursue our love, knowing the risks, or should we give up on our feelings and try to move on?

Well, we decided to continue pursuing our love, even though it's difficult and dangerous we even named the baby Thandolwethu (Our love). We found ways to spend time together, even if it is for a few minutes at a time. We cherish every moment we have together, knowing that it could be our last. We vowed to love each other no matter what, and to never give up on our love. We know our love is strong enough to overcome any obstacle. We are determined to be together even if it means going against the world.

Sibongile's ex-wife was more jealous and angrier about our relationship. She tried to sabotage our plans and made it difficult for us to be together. She was determined to ruin our happiness, no matter what it takes.

We tried to be understanding and be patient, but she was so annoying. She spread rumors about us some almost cost us our careers and tried to turn our friends against us. We started feeling isolated and alone. I began to wonder if IA it worth it to continue fighting for our love. It's not an easy decision, and we were now drained by this silly fight since she now ganged with Nick to make our lives miserable.

"If you love someone, set them free. If they come back, they are yours. If they don't, they never were." – Richard bacnch. We are now at the crossroads; we don't know what to do next. We both have families to protect. We know our love is strong, and it will overcome the obstacles in our way. Whatever happens we will always have this quote to remind us of the power of love.

Like George Bums said "Love is a lot like a backache. It doesn't show up on X-rays, but you know it's there." It's a little bit silly but it makes an important point. Sometimes love is hard to see, but it's always there, even when it's hard to explain. We may not be able to quantify our love, but we know that it's real and it's powerful.

As things went by, I realized that while I may not be able to have the life, I imagined with Sibongile, I can still create a new life for myself. A life that is full of happiness and joy. A life that is full of new experiences and new people. I know that I have a lot of living left to do. And I'm ready to embrace all that life has to offer.

After 1 year

One day my phone rang in the middle of my afternoon nap. I was tempted to ignore it, but something made me reach for the phone .it was Sibongile's number on the screen. I hesitated before answering, but I did pick up the call.

"Hello." I said.

My voice is thick with sleep.

"Hi, I was wondering if we could meet up. I have something important to tell you." He said.

My heart started racing. What could he want to tell me and why did he sound so serious?

"Sure." I said

I hung up and got off the bed, took a quick shower got dressed and headed to the coffee shop he had suggested we meet. I felt a bit nervous as I walked through the door, but I spotted him sitting at a table in the corner. He looked up when I entered, and a smile spread across his face. I felt a rush of relief and happiness at the sight of him. I took a seat across from him, and he reached out and took my hand in his.

"You look beautiful." He said.

"Thank you, you don't look bad too." I said.

We shared a laughter and he looked at me seriously. My heart was pounding in my chest.

"I have some news, and sure you're wondering why after so long. I delt with my ex-wife and she won't bother us anymore." He said.

My eyes widened in surprise. I did not expect that. I wasn't even sure what to say.

"Wow." I said.

"I know it's a lot to take in, but I wanted you to know how much I missed you, and how much you and the kids mean to me. I've been thinking a lot about our future, and I want you to be a part of it." He said.

I was speechless. I just kept looking here and there, what else could I have done.

"I know it's been hard, but I am finally free to be with you, if you will have me." He said.

My eyes filled with tears. I had been waiting for this moment for so long, and it was finally here. I took a deep breath and said

"Of course, I want to be with you. I have always loved you and I still love you and I will never stop loving you. I have been wanting for this day." I said

CHAPTER 54

*M*e *and my man sat there, holding hands and looking into each other's eyes. We were both filled with so much love and joy that it was almost overwhelming.*

"I have a question, where do we go from here. What does our future look like?" I asked.

"I think we should take things slow; we have both been through a lot, and we need to give ourselves time to heal and figure out what we want. But I think we have a bright future ahead of us." He said.

I nodded I knew that he was right, and I was glad that he was willing to take things slow. We both needed time to adjust to our new reality.

"I'd like to take you out for dinner. I know a great restaurant not too far from here. We can have a nice, romantic evening and talk about our plans." He said.

I smiled and nodded.

"That sounds perfect, let me tell Balekile I will be late today." I said.

And so, the two of us got up from our table and left the coffee shop, hand in hand, ready to start our new life together.

We arrived at the restaurant and were seated at a cozy table for two. We ordered food and chatted happily about our future. I couldn't stop smiling. I felt like I was in a dream. As we were finishing our meal, Sibongile reached into his pocket and pulled out a small, velvet box. My heart skipped a beat.

"What is this?" I asked.

"Open it and find out." He said.

Smiling, while I opened the box and saw a beautiful, sparkling diamond ring.

"Will you marry me?" He asked.

I was speechless. I had never imagined that he would propose to me so soon. But as I looked into his eyes, I knew that I wanted to spend the rest of my life with him.

"Yes…Yes I will marry you." I said.

Tears streamed down my face. My gentle guy slid the ring onto my finger and pulled me close for a kiss. The other diners in the restaurant clapped and cheered for us, we were now engaged. It was a moment I will never forget. I was starting a new chapter in my life, and I was ready to face the future with him by my side.

As we left the restaurant, hand in hand, we both knew that this was just the beginning of our journey together. We had a lot of hard work ahead of us, but we were ready to face it all. As I looked at my engagement ring. I thought about how far we had come and how much we had overcome. I felt like anything was possible, as long as we were together. And we were ready for whatever the future held for us. Our love had conquered all.

Enough about me and my husband to be, not to brag but our love is everything a girl could die for. Now we're back to Balekile. I'm actually very supportive of his and Naledi's relationship, and I get along well with her. In fact, I'm more than happy to have her as part of the family. But her parents are not supportive anymore. They don't think Balekile is no longer good enough for her and they tried to convince her to break up with him, but she refused.

On the other hand, there's a lawyer, working for a big firm in the city. He's successful and driven, but he feels like there's something missing from his life. He's always focused on his career, and he is never really taken the time to find love. Naledi's parents met with the lawyer, and they think he's the perfect match for her. He's successful and has a bright future ahead of him. They tried to persuade her to end things with my son and pursue a relationship with the lawyer instead of Balekile. The poor child is torn between her feelings for Balekile and the pressure from her parents.

Later that day Naledi decided to call Balekile and tell him about all this.

"I'm sorry, my parents are really pushing me to date the lawyer. They don't think you're the right one for me anymore." She said.

"I thought we were happy together; I don't understand why your parents would want you to date someone else. I thought they like me." He said

"I'm sorry. I wish things could be different. I care about you, but my parents are making it difficult. I don't want to disappoint them" she Said.

My poor baby was so devastated, Naledi was feeling ashamed, she knew this was never going to be easy for Balekile. But she did not know what else to do. My son was quiet for a moment.

"I wish I could make them see how much I care about you, but I understand that it's not that simple. I just don't want to lose you. And it seems as if you have already made up your mind. If you are not going to fight for this relationship, then who am I?" He said.

"I don't want to lose you either." she said.

"But I don't know what to do. I feel so stuck. I wish I had an answer for you. Maybe we need some time apart, it's not that I want to break up with you. But maybe if we take a step back, your parents will see that I'm not so bad after all." He said.

Naledi went silent for a moment. She's not sure if this was the right thing to do, but she knew that she needed to respect his wishes.

"Okay." She said.

Her voice was shaky.

"We can try being friends, but I just want you to know that I still care about you." He Said.

"I care about you too. I just want what's for you. I know this is hard, but I hope it will work out in the end." She said.

"I hope so too, maybe this is for the best. I just need some time to think. I'm sorry to miss you honestly, but I'll be here for you whenever you need me." He said.

Naledi felt a wave of sadness washing over her.

"Thank you. That means a lot to me." She said.

They said their goodbyes, and Naledi hung up the phone.

CHAPTER 55

My son was broken, I don't even know what's his next step. But all I know is that he is strong like his mom.

He took a deep breath before knocking on my door.

Knock, knock, knock.

"Come in." I said.

"Mom, can we talk, it's about Naledi." He said.

"Is everything okay?" I asked.

He took a seat on the couch.

"I want to know if I made the right decision. I took a step back from my relationship with Naledi, not because I don't care about her, but because I want what's best for her. And I think this is it." He said.

"I know you care about her." I said.

He felt a lump in his throat as he tried to speak. His eyes were teary.

"I thought she was the one, but I guess it wasn't meant to be. I thought she would make me happy, but I guess I was wrong." He said.

His voice was cracking. He looked down at his hands, feeling a wave of sadness washing over him. I put my hand on his shoulder.

"You will find someone who will make you happy, someone who is right for you. Don't give up on love just yet." I said.

He did not respond, but just nodded his head slightly.

"It is better to have loved and lost than never to have loved at all." I quoted.

My son looked up at me with a sad face and for a moment, his eyes were wet with tears.

"I know it's hard right now, but you need to take care of yourself. You can't pour from an empty cup. If you don't take care of yourself first, you won't be able to take care of anyone else." I said.

He took a deep breath. He knows I'm right, but it doesn't show it any easier.

"I just don't know what to feel better." He said.

"No baby you just need to take things easy. Like look at me I have been married to your dad my whole entire life but look at me today. I'm still standing strong. Forgive her it's not her fault you know that too. Love will visit once more." I said.

"Thank you, mama I knew you will make me feel better." He said.

I gave him a hug and tabbed him on the shoulder.

A few weeks later, Ifalethu and Thandolwethu we're visiting Mabusi. Balekile was sitting at his computer, browsing through photos of potential wedding venues. I came into the room and saw what he was doing.

"I thought we agreed to take a break from wedding planning." I said.

He signed.

"I know, but I can't help thinking about it. I feel like I need to do something to keep myself busy." He said.

"What if we just looked at venues for now. We don't have to make any decisions, but we can look at our options later when Sibongile arrives." I said.

He nodded, and we started looking through different venues online. As we were looking at the photos, my son began to feel a little bit better.

"This one look nice." He said.

Pointing to a photo of a beautiful garden.

"It has a nice outdoor space for the ceremony, and the reception hall looks spacious. It does look nice, and it's not too far from here." I said.

We looked at a few more venues then Balekile sat back in his chair.

"I think we found some good options, now we just need to narrow it down." He said.

He took a deep breath and tried to clear his head.

"I think we should start by thinking about what we want in a venue, what are our priorities?" He said.

"I think we should make sure that the venue is accessible for all of our guests. We don't want anyone to have trouble getting there." I said.

"Good point, what else?" He said.

"I think we need to make sure that the venue has good food, it's an important part of any wedding. Don't want my guests to starve." I said.

We laughed. Later on, we were watching TV, Sibongile arrived. He walked inside the house and found us on the lunch watching TV.

"Hey, how are you doing?" He asked.

Balekile looked up and smiled.

"Hey man I'm doing okay. Just watching TV took a break from browsing some wedding venues." Said Balekile.

"That's great, how's the planning going?" asked Sibongile.

"It's going to, we're visiting some progress, at least." Said Balekile.

Sibongile sat down next to me.

"Hey baby how was your day?" He asked.

"It was great my love." I said.

"Balekile, do you want to go hit the gym?" Sibongile asked.

"That sounds great! I could use a workout to clear my head." Said Balekile

"Let's go then, but let me change first, can't gym with suit on." Said Sibongile.

Balekile got up from the couch and went upstairs to grab his gym bag. My two men head out to the gym and begin their workout. As they exercised, Balekile felt his stress melting away. He felt stronger and more focused, and he started feeling better. When try finished their workout they took showers at the gym. They really can't drive sweaty. On their way to the car.

"Thanks, man that was just what I needed." Said Balekile.

The5 headed back home. Balekile took another shower then sat down at the computer again. He looked at the list of potential wedding venues and it felt a little less overwhelming.

The sun set, and we gathered around the table for dinner. Balekile sat next to Sibongile, feeling grateful for the support and encouragement. As we ate the conversation turned to wedding planning again.

"We should talk about the guest list." Said Sibongile

"Do you have any idea who you want to invite?" I asked.

"I'm thinking about inviting my close friends and family, and maybe some of the people I've met through work" he said.

While eating we made the guest list and went to bed afterwards. I now get tired of always speaking about the wedding. It's really tiring yeah, I am happy, but this is too much.

CHAPTER 56

" *When we are in love, we see the world differently, through the eyes of the heart."*

The next morning, Sibongile and I got up early, eager to start our day. It was windy and cold, but I like this kind of weather.

We had breakfast together and then headed out to his parents' house. I was so excited and nervous at the same time. It will be the first time I meet them. His parents lived in another town, and I had always wished to visit them. At his parents' house. His mom greeted us warmly, and I could see that she was happy to have us there.

"It's so good to see you both." Said his mom.

"We have been looking forward to this visit." I said

Mrs. Xaba led us in the living room, where a fire was cracking in the hearth.

We sat down, and Mrs. Xaba began to chat with us about how they have been and how much they missed their son. I told her about the wedding planning, and she offered to help in any way she could. Mr Xaba was listening, and I could see that he was not as interested in the conversation as his wife.

"So Matty what work do you do?" asked Mrs Xaba

"Actually, I have my own business." I said.

"Oh really, you are a businesswoman!" Said Mr Xaba.

"That's impressive young lady. Do you have any kids or planning to have them?" asked Mrs Xaba.

"Yes, I have two boys and 1 girl." I said.

"So many kids, where is their daddy or each has its own daddy?" he said.

"Dad, no that's not acceptable. I did not come with Matty so that you can attack her. for your own information she's a divorcee just like me." Said Sibongile.

"No dear your father did not mean it like that, please forgive him Matty. How old are your kids?" she said.

"I have 17 years old, 6 years old and 14 months old." I said.

"14 months old, and yet you have run to another man's arms." Said Mr. Xaba.

"Dad please, you know what I think it was a mistake coming here. Mom, we are leaving. Let's go Matty." He said.

"No Sibongile you don't have to leave you know how your dad is." She said.

Sibongile took my jacket and he waited for me outside. It is starting to rain, and we have to get kids from Mabusi.

"We had a really good time, thanks for having us." I said.

"Please do visit again and come with my grandchildren next time." Said Mrs. Xaba.

"Sure, we will." I said.

I hugged her and left. On our way to Mabusi's house it rained hard. We had to stop at the garage to avoid accident.

"Baby I am so sorry about what my dad said." He said.

"It's alright my love." I said.

"Really! Are we good." He said.

"Yes, we are." I said.

But honestly, I was not ok, I just felt like crying. In some time, the rain stopped, and we hit the road, few minutes we arrived. My babies we ready to go as for Thandolwethu she was so happy to see Sibongile. My baby doesn't even consider Nick as her father she says uncle and call Sibongile dad and that makes Nick sick, but he must deal with it.

We left, went to hungry lion, and ordered their wings. In no time our order came, we got in the car and went straight home. I have been so quiet all the way from my-in-laws to be house. Balekile was asleep on my couch with his sneakers on. We got in, the kids went to their rooms and changed. I helped Thando to change, this little girl is very smart. One could say she is already three years old.

I went downstairs, woke Balekile and sent him to his room he's ruining my couch. As for this one he hates his dad, the thing is after all the divorce and all he never gave them time nor called or came to check up on them. I started preparing dinner, while I was busy Mr. Xaba's words kept playing on my mind. I couldn't handle it anymore. I ran to my room and locked myself in. My man could tell I was no ok, he came to the room and knocked.

"Baby please open the door; I know you are not ok. Please don't shut me out." He said.

I know it is not his fault and I don't want to make him feel as if it is his fault. Well, he went downstairs and continued cooking. After some time, I came out, and found him busy with his little girl food tasting. I asked if I could help but they said they are fine. I went to Balekile's to check up on him, he was still asleep, just put a blanket on him and switched off the lights. When I was just closing the door on my way out, I bumped into Sibongile. He took my hand and headed to our room. Made me sit on the bed and closed the door, went on his knees, and held my hands.

"I know you are mad about what my dad said to you and it's understandable, but please don't ever give me a silent treatment ever again. It hurts to see you around where else you don't talk to me. Please forgive my dad if you can." He said.

Tears made their way out; he stood up and made me, hugged me so tight, just what I needed.

"I am sorry baby, I love you." He said.

"I love you too." I said.

He wiped my tears and kissed me.

"I don't ever want to see you cry again." He said.

I nodded and we went to have dinner. Balekile did not join us, so I put his food in the oven in case he wakes up in the middle of the night.

We had our food afterwards the kids went to bed, Sibongile read a bedtime story to Thandolwethu, and I kept myself busy with dishes. After went to my room, took and shower and we all went to sleep.

CHAPTER 57

" *T*he family is not an important thing. It's everything." - Michael J. Fox.

The following day I woke early, prepared breakfast for my people. Woke kids up, bathed Thandolwethu and Ifalethu. After that went to Balekile's room. He was deep in Sheets, I sat beside him.

"What's wrong baby are you sick" I said.

"I have this strong headache, Mama; I drank medicine I thought it will help but I'm still the same." He said.

"Aww baby, we'll go to the doctor and see what the problem could be. For now, rest I'll wake you up when I return from your brother's school." I said.

"Ok mama." He said.

I went to my room, Sibongile was still in sheets.

"Are you not going to work?" I said.

"No, I'm working home today." He said.

"OK I'm taking kids to school please look after Balekile for me, he's not doing well." I said.

"What's wrong." He said.

"Headache since yesterday, I'll take him to doctor when I return." I said.

"Ok baby." He said.

"Breakfast is ready, I'll see you now, now." I said.

Kissed him, took my car keys then left. I dropped Thandolwethu first then Ifalethu. I drove as fast as I could, reached home. Balekile was up already and ready to go. We got in the car and left to see the doctor. The doctor did a few checkups then gave him medication.

"This headache is caused by stress." Said the doctor.

"What's stressing you boy." I said.

"School, I guess and the wedding. I over worked." He said.

"Ok that could be the reason try not to work at least 2 to 3 hours a day. Just relax your mind and body." Said the doctor.

We left the hospital and went back home; he went straight to his room to take a rest. Sibongile was on the couch watching TV, I sat next to him, he put his hand around me.

"How did you go." He said.

"Great they said its stress." I said.

I got up and went to my room, took a few files, and went to office. I was just off for few days, but my shop was a total mass, Nobuhle fired the cleaner. Hair was everywhere, not to mention the towels were sticky. I called her to my office, and she gave me attitude, she forgot she's hired. She might be my cousin, but I can, and I will fire her.

"Have you seen how my shop looks. It's like pigs were living here for days. Why did you fire Maria?" I said.

"That old woman doesn't know how to talk to people." She said.

"And you know how to because you're all the same. Pack your things you're fired, find someone who's willing to do this job." I said.

She rolled her eyes and left my office, did some touch up there and there. Checked my emails, replied to some then made an announcement.

"Everyone please gathers around. As you all saw, that Nobuhle has been fired. Anyone who wants to be a manager can apply for the position but for now I'll put Rethabile as an acting manager. Rethabile please don't make me regret my decision." I said.

"No, you won't, thanks for the opportunity." She said.

"Alright, please call Maria back and tell her we need her now." I said.

Went back to my office and sat down a bit before I get to work. While facing up the door opened. It was my man. He came to my side and massaged my shoulders.

"How are you feeling now babe?" He said.

"Better thank you my love, just what I needed." I said.

"I was in the neighborhood so I thought I could surprise you with lunch. And don't worry about Balekile he's ok now, left him playing TV games." He said.

"What would I do without you. Thank you, baby, I love you. But sorry I can't eat now, have lot of work to do Nobuhle massed up big time" I said.

"What happened?" He asked.

"I'll tell you later, how about dinner tonight just the two of us in fancy restaurant at 7pm." I said.

"Sounds like a plan, and don't worry about kids I'll get them from school." He said.

"Oh, baby you're the best." I said.

He kissed me and left. I love him so much; he cares about me and loves my kids too. Around 2:47 Sibongile was already outside Ifalethu's school gate. Finally, all the kids came out, our brother here was fighting again, shirt was torn, and he was dirty as the ground. In the morning, I was called to his school because he fought and here, we are again. He got in the car and greeted me.

"Uncle please don't ask about my day today." He said.

Sibongile just laughed and drove off, then took Thandolwethu from her creche. That one was so talkative, she kept bragging about her drawing that got a star.

"Daddy is so proud of you Soulmate." He said.

That's how they call each other "Soulmate."

"Now buy me ice cream I got a star Soulmate." She said.

My baby is so close with Sibongile one could say he is her father; they go in father daughter picnics; he attends her school meetings he does everything for her.

I worked till I could take it anymore, my back started hurting, but I kept working. Around 7:30 everyone left. While working the door on the shop opened, I stood up to see who it was. Opened the office door, how did I make such a mistake?

"Baby I'm so sorry. I totally forgot." I said.

He smiled at me, put the takeaways down and hugged me.

"Since you couldn't make it to dinner it came to you." He said.

We sat down, cleared my table and started eating. We shared a moment. After eating he stood up and came to my way, started kissing me, made me sit on the table and continued kissing me. I really loved it, we made love, then locked the store and left.

CHAPTER 58

*" A baby fills a place in your heart that you never knew was empty."
- Carl Sandburg.*

We reached home and lights were off, we thought they were sleeping but nah. We got inside and here they were watching a movie on their brother's laptop.

They say it's their night movie. I had no problem with them watching a movie till night since its Friday. I went upstairs, took a quick shower then came downstairs and joined everyone.

"Have you guys eaten anything?" I said.

"Yes, Uncle Sbo cooked before leaving." Said Balekile.

I looked at him, smiled and winked at him. We watched movies till 12:30 Thandolwethu was already asleep, I took her to her room. Ifalethu asked his brother if he could sleep with him, he just wants to continue watching movies, but I refused it's late too much.

I went to my room after all kids settled, Sibongile was taking a shower, I sat on my side of the bed, took a book. He came out of the shower and got in sheets. He came close to me and hugged me, took the book out of my hand and threw it on the floor. Kissed me on the neck.

"Let's continue what we started at the salon." He said.

I giggled and action took place. The following day I felt like not getting off the bed. Sibongile was already up. I heard noises downstairs meaning all the kids were up. I woke up went to the rest room then brushed my teeth and went downstairs. Breakfast was already ready, everyone ate. Balekile seems better today.

"Are you going to work today?" said Sibongile.

"Yes." I said.

"Ok, I'm going to watch soccer with kids, your loss." He said.

"Yah! Yah! we're going out." Said Ifalethu.

"Don't be too excited Mr. fighter." I said.

I went upstairs, took a bath, wore a blue jean with white top and black sneakers, combed my afro hair and went downstairs.

"Wow mommy you look beautiful." Said Thandolwethu.

"Thank you, baby, but I always do." I said.

"Ohhh dang." Said Ifalethu.

"No Ifalethu." I said.

I knew Miss Thando will get angry, so I had to put water on fire. I took my car keys; handbag kissed my man then left. I got in the car and tried starting it, but it kept making weird noises. Called Sibongile and he came outside with his wife (Thandolwethu) beside him. He checked what problem is, but he couldn't tell What seem to be the problem. I booked a cab and went to work. When I reached there my shop was in a good condition, Maria has cleaned up and washed the towels. I greeted everyone, got to my office and got to work.

Everyone got ready for their trip to the stadium. They left, Balekile got out of the car to get tickets. On their way in they got snacks and went to sit down. On their way out they met with Nick.

"Oh, now you're fathering my kids?" He said.

"Is that necessary dude." Said Sibongile.

"Uncle Sbo you will find me in the car." Said Balekile.

"No, you guys are leaving with me." Said Nick.

"I'm not going anywhere with you. And stop saying you're my dad." Said Balekile.

"I think that's our que, let's go kids." Said Sibongile.

Nick faced down he was humiliated by what Balekile just said. Only Ifalethu loves him not sure about Balekile, but Thandolwethu is so afraid of him, she only loves his mom because she's the only person she can call grandmother. They left and went to a restaurant. They ordered and went back home. After an hour Nick came with his mom, they wanted to take the kids with them, but Sibongile refused, they caused chaos. As soon as I heard I left my workplace and came home.

They were sitting down, Ifalethu was next to his father, Balekile was sitting on the other couch alone and Thandolwethu was on Sibongile's lap. I got in and sat next to my man.

"we're here to take the kids." Said Mabusi.

"But we agreed that they visit every end of each month." I said.

"Yeah, now things have changed, I can't have kids being raised by another man, while I'm still alive." Said Nick.

"Where were you when our mom raised us alone, where were you when Ifalethu and Thandolwethu got sick, where were you. I'm not going anywhere with you. Your own child does not even know you because you were never there, the very same man you hate does what you were supposed to. If Ifa and Thando leaves with you its fine but I'm not going anywhere." Said Balekile.

We all looked at each other, my baby never poured his heart like that, he even shared a tear meaning he was really broken.

"I'm still your father Balekile you can't talk to me like that." Said Nick.

"Father, I rather not be your son, uncle Sbo please adopt me, I rather be your son than being his." He said.

He then got up and left. We were all shocked, Nick also got up and tried to go after him, but I stopped him. I asked them to leave my house because already they are confusing my kids already. They left but I bet Nick's heart was broken actually torn. He did not see this one coming. After they left, I looked at Sibongile, and ran to Balekile's room. Got inside and sat next to him, I did not say anything I hugged him so tight, and he let them out. After Some Time, I helped him get in sheets kissed him on his cheek and let him rest. When I was about to leave, he held my hand.

"Thank you, mama, I love you." He said.

"I love you too sweetheart." I said.

I left his room and went downstairs, the house was quiet, Thandolwethu was playing with her teddies and Ifalethu was playing games. Sibongile was sitting on a couch facing up, really tense. I massaged his shoulders.

"I'm sorry to drag you in my mess." I said.

"It's not your fault babe. Come sit next to me." He said.

I sat next to him and faced down the whole time.

"Matty this are my kids too, yeah I might not be their biological father but what Balekile did today showed me that your kid like me and a lot." He said.

"Thank you, for being so understanding. I love you even more." I said.

"I love you more." He said.

CHAPTER 59

" *Family is very important especially that's filled with love, care and happiness.* "

Later I started preparing dinner, but no one seemed to be interested in eating Ifalethu was mad, he says we were rude to his father. I tried talking sense into him, but he won't talk to. I went downstairs Sibongile was already on the dining table with Thandolwethu.

"I guess it's just three of us." I said.

"Yeas sit down baby and have your meal." Said Sibongile.

I lost my appetite, played with my food. It was so silent. After Thandolwethu and Sibongile finished eating I cleared the table, did the dishes while he was putting Thandolwethu to bed. After that I went upstairs and took a look hot bath. While bathing he came in, closed the toilet and sat on it.

"Hey." He said.

"Hi baby." I said.

He looked at me so quietly for a moment.

"I'm I am bad mother?" I said.

"No, you are a very good mom, actually the best. What makes you say that." He said.

"Just saying." I said.

He stood up, took a towel, and gave it to me.

"Come out I want to show you something." He said.

I got out, wiped myself and went to the bedroom, put some lotion on and wore my pj's. I sat down next to him, he held my hand and played

"I love you by Celine Dion" that lifted my spirit a bit. He took my photo with my kids and showed it to me.

"Look how happy you all look. This picture was taken way after Nick, and you got divorced then why are you doubting your love for your kids. Stop letting Nick and his mom get in your head, you're way better than this. This child loves you a lot so never doubt yourself; you are raising them so well." He said.

He looked and me and hugged me so tight.

"Thank you Xaba just what I needed." I said.

Kissed me on the forehead and we got inside sheets and slept peacefully. Around 3 am I woke up, couldn't sleep any sleep I went downstairs. Balekile was in the kitchen eating, he was starving, I guess. Greeted him, took a glass, and drank water.

"How are you feeling now?" I said.

"Better." He said.

"Ok good night baby, don't stay till late." I said.

Tabbed his shoulder and went back to my room. I tried sleeping till I don't know, when I woke up it was morning, Sibongile came with tray of food. Placed it on the bed and pulled me out the sheets to the bathroom, Gave me my toothbrush and toothpaste. I brushed my teethe while he was hugging me from behind. We went back to the bedroom, sat on the bed and had my breakfast in bed perfectly.

They say Sundays are for lovers and I say Sundays is the church day. Finally, we will be going to church. Don't remember when last I went to church but none of my kids have been to church. I got up took a shower and fit ready. Everyone was still asleep, I made breakfast for them, went through their stuff to iron their clothes. Firstly, I went to Balekile's room took out his blue shirt and black jeans and black sneakers, then Ifalethu's since he does not have shirts, he has only school shirts just taken out black SPCC t-shirt and black jeans with white sneakers. My queen here has lot of opinions, pink balloon dress or blue, but I think blue will fine with white pumps. Finally, my man, took out his favorite suit, royal blue with black shirt and white sneakers, he doesn't do sharp noses shoes.

After ironing I woke them up, they brushed their teeth then had breakfast after that they had shower.

I bathed Thandolwethu then went downstairs to wait for everyone. They were so happy to go to church they always wanted to see how it is like, what do pastors preach about. We got in the car, Balekile sat in front with Sibongile, and I Sat at the back with kids. We drove off to the nearest church. Got out of the car and went inside.

The service had not begun yet, we found ourselves sitting and waited. Ten minutes later it began, we sang and sang, pastor came in and preached the word. He was preaching about a good woman. Proverbs 31. I really enjoyed the day at church with my babies. After church we left went straight home, had prepared serve in colors. While eating.

"We really had a great time today, thanks mom." Said Ifalethu.

"I also enjoyed it. Daddy did you enjoy it?" Said Thandolwethu.

"I did my angel." He said.

"So should we go again next week?" I said.

"Yes, mommy please, please, please!" Said Ifalethu.

"Ok we will, Balekile did you enjoy?" I said.

"Yes, I did mom thanks." He said.

He was busy on his phone, I'm sure it had anything to do with a girl.

"Mommy I don't want to be a doctor anymore; I want to be a pastor." Said Ifalethu.

"Oh really!" I said.

"Ifa being a pastor is not a career it's a calling, God has to choose you to preach for us followers." Said Sibongile.

"Oh, then I want to be a doctor." He said.

We laughed and had our food; I really enjoyed this afternoon with my family. After eating I did the dishes, and everyone went upstairs to change. After doing the dishes I went upstairs, Ifalethu was playing games with his brother and Thando was playing in her doll house.

I got in my room tossed myself on the bed, Sibongile was busy with his tablet, and I didn't want to disturb him, took a towel then went to take a bath. I bathed and wore just casual clothes. Sat on the bed and tried sleeping.

"Are you tired?" He said.

"Yeah, just feel like sleeping the whole week." I said.

"Baby I have been doing some thinking, why don't we find a helper, you have a lot in your plate, you have to take care of the business, kids, chaos there's a lot." He said.

"Yeah, I could do with some help, but will you give some time to think about it?" I said.

"Take your time, and don't worry about the money, I'll be the one to pay her." He said.

That one was a relief. Yeah, I really need help, what will happen when Balekile goes to college, who will help me with dishes. I fell asleep while thinking about that.

CHAPTER 60

" *It is only with the heart that one can see rightly; what is essential is invisible to the eye." - Antoine de Saint-Exupery, The Little Prince.*

I guess I was tired; they didn't even wake me up. When I woke up the lights were off, it was so quiet in the house. Sibongile was sleeping next to me so peacefully, I reached my phone to look at the time and I could not believe it, it was 23:07. I got off the bed and went to check up on my kids. They were all sleeping. I went downstairs to see what they have ate, my poor babies ate leftovers from the meal after church. I took a deep breath and went upstairs, took off my clothes and wore pj's and got in sheets.

"Oh, you're awake, you must be hungry your food is in the oven." He said.

He was so sleepy I couldn't hear some words properly.

"No baby I'm fine, sleep my love. I love you." I said.

Hugged him and slept. The following morning, I woke up on time, brushed my teeth and went downstairs to make breakfast. I made bacon and eggs with toasted bread without butter and coffee. I did my usual routines, woke up Sibongile and kids, ironed their uniform, shoes was Balekile's Job to polish them, bathed Thandolwethu and fixed her hair. And everyone had breakfast except my man, he was still getting dressed. While eating.

"Why didn't you guys wake me up yesterday." I said.

"Uncle said we should let you rest, you're tired." Said Ifalethu

Oh, that's my man, it definitely sounds like him, he came downstairs, kissed me on a cheek and sat beside me and ate from my plate.

"How did you sleep baby." He said.

"Very well thanks my love, you. Let me fix your collar." I said

"Great." He said.

After fixing him he got up, took his laptop bag, car keys and phone.

"I'm running late, see you guys later." He said.

"Bye!" We all Said.

I also got up, took a shower, and followed him. We got in the car while Balekile was locking the house, I drove off the driveway, he got in and we left. Took him first to his school, then Thandolwethu and Ifalethu were the last because I had to meet his teacher regarding the fight on Friday. We were sitting in the waiting area with the parents of that other kid, they were so happy to see me. Don't forget I was the face of Young Empowerment to them I am the celebrity. We got inside the office of the principal; we sat down and Ifalethu Sat on my lab.

"Hello, my name is Glenda I'm your kid's English teacher and class teacher. I called you here because I want us to resolve the issue between these kids. They had a fight twice in 1 week because of a pencil. The other one says the pencil is his and the other one says so too." She said.

"Excuse me can you show us the pencil please." I said.

She showed it to us and to be honest my son was the thief.

"Ifalethu, this pencil is not yours; I don't buy you these pencils, then why did you lie." I said.

"He is the one who started it, he stole my ruler first." He said.

"You are lying, liar liar pants on fire." Said the other kid.

"I don't want to hear excuses, apologize." I said.

He tried speaking for himself, but I did not want to hear a word, finally he apologized, and they made peace. I also apologized for my son's behavior. We then left, I walked Ifalethu to his class then went to my car. That boy's parents asked to take a selfie with me, and I happily agreed little did I know. I went to the salon. Greeted and went to my office, went through my mails especially the ones for manager position, it was so difficult for me to decide.

Around lunch time I went to get Sibongile, his favorite coffee and muffins. I walked into his workplace and all eyes were on me. I asked at the front desk when I could find him, I've never been I'm his workplace before. The lady escorted me to his office she knocked and got in; he was busy on the phone. The lady closed the door I went to sit down on the couch in few minutes he was done with his call. Came to sit next to me and kissed me.

"What a lovely surprise, was just about to go out for lunch." He said.

"I just needed a reason to get out of the salon." I said.

"Ok, how's your day so far." He said.

"So tiring, oh I did go to Ifalethu's school, you won't believe it. Our son stole a pencil, this whole fight was just because of a pencil." I said.

He laughed.

"So, Ifa just decided to steal, just like that." He said.

"No, he says that boy stole his ruler first so the whole pencil thing was just a revenge." I said.

"Yeah eish, kids. But is everything OK now." He said.

"Yeah, they're good." I said.

We had our food then I left, he walked me out of his office. While going out of the building everyone was looking at me, I'm used to the attention, but this one was weird. I even thought I had something on my face, took my phone out to check what's wrong with me but I saw nothing. Walked to my car and sat a bit before driving. The very same thing happened again when I walked in my salon. I went to my office called Rethabile and asked her what's wrong with people staring at me. She took her phone out and showed me a picture of me and the parents of the boy Ifalethu fought with. The caption said.

"She maybe smart, beautiful and rich but her son is a thief."

I gave her phone, and she left my office, I could not believe, but none the less I'll meet them later. I continued with my work. While working my phone rang and it was Sibongile.

"Baby." I said.

"Are you Ok? My colleague just showed me the post about you." He said.

"I'm alright my love, I'll fix it later when I get Ifalethu from school." I said.

"Don't you want me to come with you?" He said.

"No, I'll be fine, I'm a big girl." I said.

"Ok I love you." He said.

"I love you too." I said.

I hung up and continued with my work.

CHAPTER 61

" *We've created a world where the truth is in the eye of the beholder." - Charles F. Glassman.*

As time went fast as I wanted it to be, I grabbed my handbag, car keys and Phone and went to Ifalethu's school. Only 5 minutes had left till the school bell rang.

I sat in the car and waited. It rang, I sat quietly in my car. I saw Ifalethu coming, I got out of the car grabbed his hand and went back inside the school with him, grabbed the other boy's hand too and went to their class teacher, they sat down, I showed her the post.

"This is really bad, why would they do that? Let me call them." She said.

"Don't let them I'm here they might send someone." I said.

She called them and they Said they're just outside the gate they're coming now, I also wanted the principal to be called and he did come. When they got in, they were shocked to see me, they looked here and there. Their son tried running to them, but I held him back.

"How could you guys, why acting so childish, what you're doing could ruin my business do you know that?" I said.

"Why you did was unacceptable, why didn't you mention that your son also stole a ruler, no wonder why your kid behaves the way he does, he inherits it from you. I'm so disappointed Mrs. Khumalo." Said the principal.

I let go of their son, they looked at me with shame.

"You better get rid of that post, or you'll know who I am. I'll give you the reason to post about me." I said.

Took Ifa and left, I have never been so annoyed. I picked up all the kids, but as usual Balekile walked home. In no time we reached, went upstairs to change then made some sandwiches. While eating I took my phone and texted Sibongile.

"I took care of that matter." I said.

Later I cooked dinner, Sibongile arrived freshened up and we all ate. After everyone went to their room, Sibongile put Thandolwethu to bed then went to our room. I cleaned the table and did the dishes then went to my room. I wore pj's, sat on the bed. He was reading a book, so I just put on some lotion on my feet then got in sheets. Kissed him on the cheek, switched off the light on my side then slept.

It was a cool and normal morning; I got ready since I have somewhere important to be. The kids were downstairs with Sibongile having breakfast ready to go so Sibongile dropped them. Today was the most important day of my life, my wedding dress fitting. So, I went to the shops to get a few things first then went to the fitting.

Well, it was a magical moment during the fitting, tears made their way out my cheek when I saw myself on the mirror, it felt as if I was the bride already. My dress was so beautiful, the fabric flows gracefully as I move, and it was smooth. It was classic with fitted bodice; the color was creamy white and soft with sparkle and diamonds on the cleavage.

The wedding was in 3 days, Balekile had found the venue already, so I don't have a lot on my plate. I took Sibongile and the kids suits not to forget the flower girl's dress. We are not going to have a big wedding since we both had been married first. We just going to invite 50 people including families.

After all that I went home, Balekile was home already, his schoolteachers had workshop, so the school was out early. He helped me unpack all the groceries, gave him his suit to fit it in and it was suiting him perfectly. I texted Sibongile told him I got the suits and come home early. It's his last day today at work since he took a leave. Around two- thirty Balekile took the car keys and went to get his siblings from their schools.

As for Nick life was bit difficult for him. Mabusi was not Ok physically, and Jack was too busy with work. Nick started working with his mom again but not the same position he was when he got fired. Well, he was expecting another child so he couldn't cope without his other kids, especially with Balekile's despise towards him and Thandolwethu not knowing he's her father despite tell her the truth she doesn't want to believe and she's just a child we can't force her.

Well, the kids arrived I already made food for them. Thando came running to me.

"Big brother told me and small brother you got suit for him! What did you get for us?" she said.

"Hi to you too Thandolwethu, I got you nothing." I said.

Her eyes started being teary, she folded her arms and looked at her brothers. I laughed.

"Go upstairs change and come have your meal." I said.

She went downstairs with her brother, changed and came back downstairs. They had their meal while Balekile was busy finalizing things at the venue, and I was sending the invitations. They ate and joined us in the sitting room. They watched the cartoons for some time then went outside to play. Everything seemed perfect, catering people were not yet paid but Sibongile said he will take care of that.

Around five pm Sibongile arrived, he forgot he had to get his parents, but they really can't stay here, but I did not know how I'll break that to him. When he arrived, he went upstairs, and I joined him. Hugged him from behind.

"How was your day? "I asked.

"Great, I'm glad I have two months to myself." He said.

"Lucky you." I said.

We went silent for a moment; he was busy taking off the suits and wore short pants and white shirts with no shoes on. I sat on the bed and cleared my throat.

"Uhm babe do you remember you have to get your parents." I said.

"Yeah, I remember, we'll get them late want to rest a bit." He said.

"Ok baby don't get me wrong but I don't think your parents should be staying here." I said

I looked at my hands and he looked at me as if he I said something wrong.

"I said don't get me wrong. The last thing I want is your father insulting us. Don't want him to say you stay at the other man's house, you know how he can be." I said.

He sat next to me and held my hand.

"I understand but this house is yours right and he won't know Nick had stayed here when you guys were married." He said.

"Are you sure?" I asked.

"Yes, don't worry I'll deal with my father you have nothing to worry about." He said.

It was a relief to hear him saying that. His father can sometimes be a real pain in the ass. We went downstairs to finish up the wedding preparations.

CHAPTER 62

" *When a man marries, he's entitled to forsake his mother and father, but he's not entitled to forget them*" - Samuel Butler.

Later Sibongile and I went to his parents' house to get them. From our place to there I was doing a serious prayer in my heart for his father. We knocked at the door and got inside. His mom welcomed us so warmly, she gave us their bags since it was late already. His father was at the back feeding his chicken He reminded me of my uncle we would wait for the while thirty minutes for him while he feeds his chicken and dog's. Well finally we left and stopped at the mall to get few things for them.

Finally, we arrived, Ifalethu was playing TV games in Balekile's bedroom, Thandolwethu was playing with her dolls in her bedroom as for Balekile was watching news. Well, we got in and I unpacked things, Mr. and Mrs. Xaba joined Balekile they greeted him, and he greeted back. Sibongile went upstairs to call the others. They came down, they greeted and sat down.

I was busy in the kitchen making tea, Mrs. Xaba came.

"You have a very beautiful house." She said.

"Thank you, Ma." I said.

I took the tray and went to the sitting room. MaXaba sat down and had her tea. My kids went upstairs to play games. I sat down next to Sibongile and held his hand.

"You taught your son very well Matty, he is my favorite from now." Said Mr. Xaba.

"What do you mean dad?" said Sibongile.

"I mean not many youths watch the news these days more over he took his siblings upstairs when he saw all adults sat down. He's very respectful I like him." He said.

"Thank you, I really try to raise them with respect." I said.

"Yeah, you are doing a very good job." He said.

"So how are the wedding preparations?" said Maxaba.

"Everything is fine. We are just waiting for the big day." I said.

We all smiled and shared a very calming conversation, I never saw that side of Mr. Xaba before, I must say he really likes Balekile actually he really liked my kids. Later I was upstairs with Sibongile in our room looking at some pictures on the internet. Thandolwethu came running saying Ifalethu is not Ok. I quickly got up and went to his room. He has rush all around his body.

"What did you eat Ifa. Take off the clothes I'll apply something on your skin, baby please get some cloves." I said.

"I ate chocolate, but I didn't know it has peanuts." He said.

"No Ifalethu I told you to never eat chocolate, didn't I?" I said.

"Sorry mom." He said.

I applied some cream on him, Sibongile rushed to the chemist to get few things for him. This can't be happening, it's only few days before the big day. I have waited for this day so long I really can't wait anymore. After applying cream, he slept, and I got ready to prepare dinner.

Maxaba joined me while cooking, her husband was resting in their room. Well, she helped me here and there. When dinner was ready, I dished some for Ifalethu and took it to his room, asked others to join us. Ifalethu can't e with us. Thandolwethu might get sick too so to be safe he has to stay in his room. We all ate after I did the dishes with Balekile. Since and his parents were watching TV Thandolwethu went to bed.

"I really like Matty, she's not bad as I thought. You knew how to choose son." Said Mr. Xaba.

Sibongile looked and his dad then his mom. He couldn't believe it's his father who said those words. He really gave me hard time.

"I told you dad, Matty is nice and not just nice decent too and respectful." Said Sibongile.

After doing the dishes my baby went upstairs to rest too and I checked on Ifalethu. He was also asleep. Sent his teacher a text already,

I'm taking him to the doctor tomorrow. Went downstairs to join Sibongile and his parents but he was alone, they had already gone to bed. We went to our room and had a shower together then went to bed.

"Happiness is not a station you arrive at, but a manner of traveling." – Margaret Lee Runbeck. This quite means happiness is not a destination but rather a way of expressing life. It's not something you achieve once.

The following day I woke up early had to prepare Thandolwethu first then Ifalethu. After getting ready they ate and Sibongile dropped Thandolwethu and Balekile at their schools. I took Ifalethu to the doctor. Before leaving I told Maxaba where I put their breakfast.

Well, I reached at the doctor, he did few check ups. And gave him medication. Luckily, they say he will be better by tomorrow at least I will enjoy my day. I went to the mall and got few things for him then went home. Maxaba was making lunch, Sibongile and his dad were outside in the back yard watering plants. I took Ifalethu to his room, changed his sheets and gave him his medication.

I went downstairs helped Maxaba set the table. I then went outside to call Sibongile and his father for lunch.

"Greetings Mr. Xaba how did you sleep?" I asked.

"I slept very well thank you my child." He said.

"When did you get back babe?" Asked Sibongile.

"Not so long, lunch is ready." I said.

"Ok we are coming now, now." Said Mr. Xaba.

I went inside sat down with Maxaba with the conversation going, while waiting Sibongile and his dad joined us. While eating.

"Uhm Matty my child." Said Mr. Xaba.

"Yes." I said.

"I really don't know where to start. I want to apologize for my behavior towards you in these past months, I was really harsh towards you." He said.

"It is all in the past now." I said.

"Forgiveness is the fragrance that the violent sheds on the heel that has crushed it." - *Mark Twain.*

Forgiveness is beautiful and powerful, even if someone has hurt you, they can be forgiven. It will not be easy but it's worth it in the end.

CHAPTER 63

" *A successful marriage requires falling in love many times, always with the same person." - Mignon McLaughlin.*

This means love is not just a one-time thing, but something that has to be nurtured and rekindled over and over again. Well, the wedding day has finally arrived the day I have been dreaming about, I have never been so sure about anything like this in my life. I could feel from my bones that Sibongile is the one. The love he showers me with give me no space to doubt him. This was my chance to start a new chapter filled with happiness and love.

Like Mahatma Gandhi said, "Where there is love, there is life." I was so beautiful no words can explain how beautiful I was looking. As for my entrance it was heart melting, before walking down the aisle I asked the DJ to play the recording that I made it said.

"Dear Sibongile, on this special day, I want to let you know how important you are to me. You are my rock, my bestie more over the love of my life. I consider myself lucky to have you in my life and to be able to spend the rest of my life with you, thank you for choosing me to be your life partner and thank you for being you. I love you with all my heart."

After that recording, they played my favourite song "I do" by Amanda Black. The wedding I was having is my dream wedding, I fooled myself when I thought my first wedding was my dream wedding. I bet this one was to die for. When I walked down the aisle Sibongile had tears on his cheeks I believe it was tears of joy. His heart was full of love and joy as he sees how beautiful I was, it was written all over his face.

I stood in front of him, and I wiped his tears, but they could not stop falling. I held his hands and Pastor started the ceremony. The garden was filled with the sweet scent of flowers, sun rays streamed trough the tress, our wedding was at Botanical Garden. The guests were happy. My heart was pacing.

"Dearly beloved, we are all gathered here to celebrate the union of this woman and this man. They decided to unit their families and join their lives together. We are all here to celebrate and witness their love. May their love blossom with each passing day and always cherish bond they are forming today. So Sibongile you now can say your vows." Said the Pastor.

"I stand before you today, not as a perfect man, but as a man who is willing to love you for the rest of our lives, I promise to stand by you on your worst times and celebrate with you in times of joy. I will be your confident, lover, friend and partner in all things. I promise to cherish you, honer you, respect you and love you, mostly support you throughout our lives." He said.

My eyes were filled with tears upon hearing all of that. Well, my turn came, I did not write mine down but just said what is in my heart.

"I vow to love you and take care of you for the rest of our lives. I promise to be your partner in all things, through good and bad times. I will support you, cherish you, encourage you and stand by you all times, no matter what life throw our way. With you by my side all is possible, thank you for choosing me to be your wife." I said.

"Beloved as we can all see, this two knows the real true meaning of love, for now is there anyone who says this two should not get married?" He said.

I looked at our guest smiling, I was at peace till my eyes saw Nick and his mom. My heart started racing but no one stood up, I really thought he's going to cause trouble for me but not so the pastor continued.

"So Sibongile do you take Matty as your beloved wedded Wife?" Pastor asked.

"I do." He said.

"Matty, do you take Sibongile as your wedded Husband?" He asked.

"I do." I said.

Even before the pastor said you may kiss the bride Sibongile was all over me. During the reception we shared a very romantic moment, we even danced our first dance as husband and wife, all over each other and staring in each other's eyes. We cut the cake and fed each other a piece of it with smile. Oh, the food, they were beautifully presented, and it tasted good than it seems. There was meat and vegetables to delicate pastries and mouth-watering desserts. The meal was traditional and certifying.

The beauty of our wedding was incredible. Everything was perfect from my entrance to the after party. It was the day to be remembered forever, a day when happiness was all around, and love was in the air. This is my perfect day.

As for our honeymoon, it was in Cape Town. We explored the city, did the mountain hiking and other things. Our honeymoon was a once off experience, we enjoyed it, and I am never forgetting the beauty of Cape Town. After the weekend we retuned. Our Life after marriage had a real turn and it was a good one trusts me. Sibongile got the promotion at Dubai, so we had to relocate, we got schools for the kids, and we started our lives afresh. I knew our future was promising. As my man and I walked hand in hand with our kids into the future, I knew whatever comes our way we will face it together. We lived happily ever after not because we did not have problems but because we faced our problems together. Our deepest sorrow we had our way of leading happy tomorrow.

Like Fawn Weaver said "Happily ever after is not a fairy tale but it is a choice." But our love story was a fairy tale.

©

THE END

www.ingramcontent.com/pod-product-compliance
Lightning Source LLC
Chambersburg PA
CBHW071152170626
46809CB00002B/865